Spirit Gift

A journey through the seven planes of existence

By
Jeff Wellman

Praise for Spirit Gift

As an end-of-life doula, I found "Spirit Gift" to be an insightful and beautiful perspective not only on finding meaning to life, but a deeply thought-provoking peek into life after death as well. Its lessons have brought more self-awareness into my own life, and have enriched my understanding of the Spirit world.

Angela Shook
End-of-Life Doula
Past president, National End-of-Life Doula Alliance
Instructor, End-of-Life Doula Professional Certificate Program, University of Vermont

Wellman takes readers on an existential journey with Qaletaqa, the Native American protagonist who goes through inspirational changes in his pursuit of enlightenment. A well told narrative, *Spirit Gift* is a simple yet motivational odyssey

Steve Miller, journalist and author, *Detroit Rock City: The Uncensored History of Rock 'n' Roll in America's Loudest City.*

OUTSTANDING!!! WOW! This simple yet profound story is wonderfully told to be most enjoyable and revealing of great spiritual truths. It gives hope and enlightenment to the reader. It truly is and will be a blessing to many.

Reverend, Pat Crawford
President & Medium at Snowflake Spiritualist Church Camp

Better World Publishing
Waialua, HI 96791

Copyright © 2023 Jeff Wellman
All rights reserved.

No part of this book may be reproduced in whole or in part or transmitted in any form or by any means, electronic or mechanical, including photocopying, recording, or by any information storage and retrieval system, without the written permission of Diane Button or Better World Publishing, except where permitted by law.

Cover & Interior Design & Composition: Ehukai Marketing

Available Internationally on Amazon European websites.

Library of Congress Cataloging-in-Publication Data
    Wellman, Jeffrey Allen, 1960–
    Sprit Gift, – *A journey through the seven planes of existence* / Jeff Wellman. p. cm.
    LCCN: 2023903308

ISBN: 979-8-9850646-3-6

The corporate mission of Better World Publishing is: *Inspiring lives of passion and service for a better world.*

FIRST EDITION
Copyright © 2023 Jeff Wellman

All rights reserved.

In memory

... of Julie Wellman, for your passion and Spirit. Your continued help and guidance from the Spirit world has helped me immensely and awed me completely. Your warmth, love, and patience over thirty-two years will never be forgotten. Thank you for teaching me and convincing me that there is so much more beyond this physical world we call Earth.

Foreword

I didn't write this book! Yes, I put pen to paper, but the inspiration, storyline, and truths from the Spirit world all came from Spirit guides during serene meditation.

I was introduced to meditation forty years ago while practicing martial arts. As a young, high-strung, Type-A business salesperson, I dismissed the idea that meditation could ever help me. I couldn't sit still and calm my mind for one minute let alone several hours. Not to mention, I was too busy for that nonsense.
Luckily, my instructors implored me to try it in small doses and keep extending my time in consciousness. It was arduous, but I persisted and began to see the difference meditation made in my life.

Today I can transcend into a quiet meditative state quickly and for hours at a time. Meditation has changed my life, made me a better person all around, and created this book.

I'm not sure why Spirit guides chose me to share this message with the world, but I'm grateful. Their knowledge and guidance awe me and continue to help me live a better life.

Spirit guides shared the concept of this book with me during quiet meditation on the Big Island of Hawaii. My wife and I were vacationing at the Kona Sheraton Resort. I started each day meditating from a natural seat carved out of the black lava cliff over crashing ocean surf. There, a manuscript took shape in my mind, then over several years and countless hours of meditation, it became this book that I am proud to share with you.

Author's Note

This story is my interpretation of insights from Spiritual masters of the present and past. Insights from visionaries like Buddha, Deepak Chopra, Ramdas, and other Yogis. They share visions of Spiritual planes and life after our brief Earth adventure, along with life lessons we all need to enjoy an extraordinary existence.

I chose a time frame for this story, 1211, when there was no organized religion. No one to taint or mold our beliefs and Spirit. The only people in the area were the indigenous, original people. They were, and are to this day, very Spiritual people. Their true Spirit comes from their hearts and souls, not books or preaching.

As a white male, I won't pretend to know their culture as intimately as their own people. I have studied this beautiful culture in our local libraries, read articles and books from their own resource center, and consulted with the native people of the area. They are very Spiritual people and have always understood that life continues indefinitely.

That is the core value of this book, along with lessons one can use to live a joyful life of peace and harmony.

I'd like to thank Julie for gently pushing me to finish this book and get it out to the world. Your nudging me along while on earth and even more so from heaven has inspired me to no end. You were a force on the earth plane and even more so from the Spirit world. Thank you for bringing my Spirit guides to help me with this project.

My new love and wife, Angela, has inspired me as well. You met my endless questions with love and patience.

Thank you to my children, Tyler, Claire, and Madison, for allowing me the time to concentrate on the book when I should have been hanging with you. I love you so much.

Thank you to my wonderful editors, Steve Miller, Diane Button, Carrie Bolin, and Stephanie Clark, for all your hard work to make me look like I knew what I was doing.

Thank you to my Vice President-do all, Deb Jason, for coaching me through the trials and tribulations of the Microsoft Word program that makes no sense to me. And to Better World Publishing for helping me get off my ass and get the book out there.

You're all the best.

Contents

1.	Restless Warrior	13
2.	Aki	29
3.	Peril	37
4.	The Light	43
5.	Furious	53
6.	Spiritual Planes	59
7.	Follow Your Heart	71
8.	The Final Plane of Existence	81
9.	Returning	97
10.	Keep the Light	115
11.	Eleven Truths	121
12.	Let Love Fill Your Heart	137
13.	Breath of Life	149
14.	Spirit Teacher	163
15.	Trouble	179
16.	Tracked	189
17.	Destiny	201
18.	Okwi	207
19.	Home	211
20.	Epilogue	221
	Appendix	235

Life

Life is a human experience until death.

Death is a part of life until entering the light.

Light is your connection to source.

Source is all life.

The only question is, why are you here?

— Jeff Wellman

Chapter 1
Restless Warrior

1211, A.D.

Qaletaqa could sense the danger before he saw the timber wolf emerge from the brush behind him. It stood five feet high at the shoulders with its ears back, its cold yellow eyes staring directly at him. The smell of the entrails from the elk he had just killed enticed the predator.

The young man knew to move slowly while the gray wolf circled him. The fur at its neck stood up in attention. Qaletaqa sheathed his knife and removed the bow from around his body and shoulder. The beast stopped and eyed the hunter, then sauntered forward. The alluring scent of the kill encouraged the wolf as it moved to steal the carcass. This man was in the way, and the wolf saw him as a minor obstacle to its next meal.

It all happened quickly.

The wolf lunged. Qaletaqa pulled an arrow from his quiver, set his bow, and fired into the middle of the animal's chest. The lack of movement told Qaletaqa his shot had found its mark. Few men could have acted with the calm precision that Qaletaqa displayed. Years of hunting for his tribe in the thick Northern Michigan woods had prepared him for these extreme situations. He cautiously approached the prone wolf with his knife in hand. As he approached the animal, Qaletaqa could see the wolf breathing slowly. The last bit of life was draining from the beast, the ground beneath it turning crimson red with blood. Qaletaqa was drawn to the animal's eyes. He saw something that startled him deeply in the large, dimming pools of the wolf's eyes. There was a sense of recognition as the wolf's eyelids slowly closed. Qaletaqa brushed away the strange feeling coursing through his mind. After all, this was just a wolf.

Thankful that he didn't have to finish off the animal with his knife, Qaletaqa knelt on the soft warm earth in front of the creature; he closed his eyes and asked for forgiveness from the Great Spirit for sending such a beautiful creation to the land beyond. Qaletaqa could remember how his father spoke about respecting and caring for all living beings.

"All living things, from animals to plants and trees, have Spirits and should always be treated as equals to you. We call this Manitou," his father had shared with him many times. It was an important lesson passed through their people.

Unfortunately, life in the wilderness often forces one to make a harsh choice between life and death. If Qaletaqa felt unsafe or that danger was near, he would always choose his life above others.

Qaletaqa carefully removed the front quarters of the elk with his knife, separating it into smaller portions he would take back to the tribe. He then raised the remainder of the elk into a nearby tree. He secured the carcass with netting made of wild grapevines and hemp. Qaletaqa tied a rope to the net, threw one end over a high pine branch, and then yanked on the other until the animal was high enough to keep it away. The wolves, coyotes, and badgers would smell the meat and bones and inevitably be drawn to the scent. It would be safe until he could send a hunting party back to retrieve it. There was just too much animal here for him to carry alone.

Qaletaqa hoisted the front of the great animal over his head and shoulders. With one arm, he dragged the wolf behind. From hunting, fishing, gathering wood, and wrestling with his brothers, he had developed incredible strength. His body was quite muscular at his young age. He was the envy of the tribe's men and the desire of many of the tribe's women.

He was well-liked in his tribe and knew he could become a great warrior like his father. He wasn't egotistical but did enjoy how he felt when others congratulated him on his hunt or when others admitted defeat after a wrestling match. It made him feel proud and respected.

Every muscle strained as he began his journey back home. It was a heavy burden, and Qaletaqa had to stop often to rest. But the excitement of bringing these rewards back to his village kept him moving.

***

Their village was located on the northern shore of Pine Lake, later known as Lake Charlevoix, in the northwest reaches of Michigan's lower peninsula. With anxiety, Qaletaqa entered the hut of Chief Owosso. He knew he should not have ventured so far from the tribe, but the hunt had gotten the better of him. His absence while tracking the solitary elk for two days had the entire tribe concerned for his life. His return to the tribe sparked cheers and yelps from the young and old. Everyone was eager to hear stories of the great hunt that Qaletaqa endured. Astonished, his fellow tribespeople stared as he lumbered in with half an elk draped across his strong shoulders and a slain timber wolf dragged by its massive back paws.

Outside Chief Owosso's hut, Qaletaqa dropped the animals to demonstrate his success during his prolonged absence.

"You have been reckless," Chief Owosso said. "Many were worried. Many thought you would not return this time. Yet you return from what looks like a great hunt. Your mother worries about you. I'm sure your father even worries from the Spirit world beyond."

Qaletaqa didn't have much patience for the Chief's lectures or talks of the Spirit world beyond, but he didn't dare show it. Respect for all elders in the tribe, especially the Chief, was among the first lessons taught to the young children.

Chief Owosso regularly mentioned Qaletaqa's father. A great warrior, he said, and an even better hunter. However, the Chief never elaborated on how or when his father was taken to the Spirit world. Qaletaqa heard whispers and hushed stories of a great bear that took his father's life and how his father sacrificed himself for the entire tribe. But no one gave any detail on what happened. Qaletaqa was just too young to remember the great warrior of the tribe, his father.

"Let us talk of your future," said the Chief. "Come and sit around my fire, and we will learn what the Great Spirit has in store for you, Qaletaqa."

Qaletaqa bowed his head in respect and did as he was asked.

He spent the remainder of the day listening to Chief Owosso speak of great Manidogs—Spirits—and lands beyond the limitless boundaries of their conscious awareness. None of this talk kept his interest until the Chief told him he would be sent alone into the northern woods so his guardian Manidog could direct him in life.

Whatever that means, Qaletaqa mused to himself. It wasn't that he didn't care about his future; he just didn't want to deal with it right now. He was young and he provided for the tribe, already giving him a good sense of purpose. He didn't need direction from a Spirit.

"You have a gift inside of you, Qaletaqa," Chief Owosso said with hope. "Many don't know what their gift is until life shows them. Some figure out their gift halfway through life. Few realize their gift very early in life." Chief Owosso stared at Qaletaqa, trying to decipher his thoughts. Qaletaqa didn't seem interested in what he was being told.

The Chief worried about Qaletaqa. He knew Qaletaqa was determined to become a strong warrior. That was acceptable, but was he doing it to become just like his father, or was this his true gift and purpose for this life? Chief Owosso knew that this journey would be a great experience for Qaletaqa, and perhaps he would learn something along the way.

"The lucky ones know their purpose and share their gift with others," Chief Owosso continued. "This makes life easier for them and helps the tribe and others outside our small circle."

Qaletaqa didn't see the point in any of this. Why did he need the Manidog to guide him? Why did he have to leave the tribe? He was happy and had a great life here. Why did he need to change that?

"It is up to you how long it will take, and it may not happen at all, but you must allow yourself to find your gift," Chief Owosso spoke softly. "Reflect quietly upon yourself while you are alone on your journey. The great Manidog will help you find your way."

Qaletaqa wasn't sure what this journey would entail or if it would even work. He found rituals like this ridiculous and archaic. But he would still go to make the tribe happy. Whether it would work or not was the real question.

***

Qaletaqa stayed at home with his mother, Okwi, and his brothers for the subsequent two days. He readied himself for his journey between bouts of wrestling with his brothers, spear-throwing games, and pondering why he had to leave the tribe at all. He was confused about what the Chief meant when he talked about "finding yourself."

When young men reached eighteen, they were required to spend a year living in the wilderness to discover who they were and what they wanted out of life. Qaletaqa didn't really agree with the tradition. It seemed like a waste of time, especially for him, who already knew his future.

He had seen plenty of young men leave and come back with stories, but no one had ever had a life-changing experience. There were times when the men never returned, and their families endured periods of sadness and despair.

Those times left a dark cloud over the tribe, as they all silently knew that the young man would not return. The words were never spoken by the tribe, but it was something that they all acknowledged.

He started preparing for his trip by packing his things. Even though he was perfectly capable of packing his belongings independently, his mother insisted on helping him. She wished to spend time with her son before he embarked on his journey because she was aware that some never returned. She wished with all her heart that Qaletaqa would come back to her safely. After suffering the loss of her true love, Qaletaqa's father, she could not take another devastating blow.

Qaletaqa bemoaned that there was not enough space in his canoe for all these provisions as he watched her work diligently and in silence to pack grains, beans, smoked fish, and dried meats. She paid him no attention and continued to add to the growing pile.

While his mother fussed with the packing, Qaletaqa took pride in sharing his most recent adventure, the slaying of the wolf and his elk kill, with his friends and younger tribe members. The village's families resided in a wide clearing on the north shore of the lake, surrounded by aged, broad hemlock pines. Twenty-one wigwams, constructed of saplings woven together and then covered in braided grass and birch bark, housed the seventy-five tribe members.

***

Qaletaqa's tribe called itself Migisi, or Eagle. The tribespeople were proud to carry the name of the Migisi because they considered themselves confident hunters and cunning fishermen, just like their namesake. They were equally proud of their young members, and took pride in sharing great hunting stories of their bravery. Qaletaqa was excited to share his.

Many children and young adults were willing to listen to Qaletaqa's hunt stories.

"How did you kill the wolf?" one young boy asked. All the young tribe members gathered around Qaletaqa to hear the tale from their favorite young warrior.

Qaletaqa waited while everyone sat in a tight circle. Once settled, they became quiet. Qaletaqa enjoyed the tense silence, with all eyes on him to begin his story.

He waited a few seconds to increase the anticipation.

"I felt the energy of the beast coming up behind me before I saw it," he told them, his voice steady and controlled. "As I turned, the brush began to move. Then I saw its large, yellow eyes staring me down. I could feel those eyes wanting to tear the flesh from my body. Then I saw its teeth. They were longer than eagle claws and dripping with saliva."

Qaletaqa paused. He had everyone's undivided attention. He suddenly jumped forward with hands stretched out in front of him like the enormous paws of a wolf.

His followers jumped and screamed.

He smirked with enjoyment. "I knew I had only one shot before it leaped on top of me and tore my neck open with those jagged fangs. I quivered my arrow and fired, piercing the wolf's heart as it soared toward me. The wolf was dead before it hit the ground."

The youngsters screamed with delight. Qaletaqa smiled. He was a natural storyteller, a true kiktowenene—speaker for his clan—and loved sharing his adventures. He enjoyed seeing his audience enthralled by his words and was gratified that they understood the majesty of his accomplishment. He might have embellished how quickly the wolf died, but he did not want to discuss the strange feeling he felt when looking at it.

Even after all this time, his reaction continued to make him uneasy. The eyes of the wolf held a sense of recognition for something. He could not recall ever having that sensation before. It was as if Qaletaqa was familiar with the Spirit that resided within. While adrenaline coursed through his body, it was easy to brush it off, but looking back on it now, it was still unsettling.

He had not abandoned his unshakable faith in the great Spirits surrounding them. When he was young, his parents and other adults shared their knowledge with him. But until today, he had never felt the presence of a Spirit quite so strongly. He pondered in his own head whether this trip would turn out to be such a terrible experience after all.

***

The following day, just as the sun rose, Qaletaqa set out on his journey. His face was painted with primary hues to prepare for this one-of-a-kind adventure. It looked like he had large teeth because he had one black stripe from ear to ear over the bridge of his nose and three smaller white stripes cascading down each cheek. During his travels, he was confident that these stripes would shield him from the influence of malevolent Spirits. Because of the sun's warmth, the only piece of clothing he required was a breechcloth, which consisted of a strip of animal hide that covered his front and back and was held in place by a woven belt.

His canoe was so heavily laden with supplies, it was difficult for him to even get it into the water, let alone maintain its upright position once it was there. His mother had filled and packed birch bark containers with wild rice, berries, nuts, leeks, corn, and squash.

For the chilly winter nights in the north, she ensured he had extra furs to keep him warm. Although it appeared as though the heavy load was going to be a burden for him, he would later be very grateful to his mother for insisting he carry it. Because of the large quantity of supplies, he would be kept warm, dry, and fed.

On the beach, the entire tribe gathered to wish him well and send him their best wishes. Qaletaqa made his way to his canoe after being greeted with hugs, tears, and cheers by his friends and family. As the younger men pulled the heavily laden boat to deeper water for him, he bid his friends and family a tearful farewell.

Paddling westward, he made his way deeper into Pine Lake. He could make good time because the large body of inland water showed no signs of ripples. As he stealthily moved along the shore, he could smell the crisp pine aroma that the towering hemlock trees gave off, and he had a distinct impression that they were protecting him. It made him happy to see cliffs of crimson rock interspersed with sandy bays. The fresh water was so transparent that you could see small fish swimming thirty feet below the surface. This spot served as his playground throughout the years, and he often spent time here frolicking with his friends and brothers and even a pretty female from time to time. The scorching sun on this picture-perfect day brought back memories of peaceful times spent lazing away on a warm sandy beach, getting some much-needed rest in between sessions of hunting, fishing, and simply having fun.

Now, he was concerned about how long he would be away from his family and friends. According to what he had learned from previous expeditions, this would take quite a long time. It took some people many years to complete the mission that they had been given. The person who returned from their individual journey the quickest did so after an entire summer season had passed. They quickly connected with their Spirit and were immersed in its teachings.

Before this, Qaletaqa had never been absent from his tribe for longer than two weeks. Since he was almost always part of a hunting party, he was never out there alone. The most extended amount of time he stayed by himself in the forest was three days. He was only there for that long because a severe storm had just passed, making it impossible for him to travel safely.

While paddling, he spent a lot of time thinking about whether or not this trip was necessary. After all, he was a hardy and courageous man who looked out for his family and ensured everyone had enough to eat. He could not fathom why the Chief would have him go on this adventure. However, everyone, including his mother, insisted it was essential.

Fine, he thought. *I'll venture out for a few months, then return and exclaim, "I found myself! Yeah!" Whatever! Who cares? Would they know if I was lying?*

Qaletaqa could not deny the thrill coursing through him, however. He loved adventure, and now there was no one to tell him what to do. Every day was his to choose. If he felt like traveling, he would travel. If he felt like fishing, he would fish. If he wanted to go hunting, he would hunt.

And if I feel like doing nothing, I will do nothing. This thought brought a smile to his chiseled features.

He paddled on.

His objective was to arrive at the beach of Mishigami. This massive inland freshwater lake would eventually turn into Lake Michigan. When the lake shrank into a small fjord and turned into a river, Qaletaqa had to portage his canoe, dragging it over logs, rocks, and beaver dams. Every muscle in his body was stretched to its limit as the loaded canoe's weight pulled it down. His back hurt, his shoulders ached, and his legs trembled.

He fought through the winding river for a full two days. On the morning of the third day, Qaletaqa could make out the sound of waves crashing against the shore of the Mishigami. He was looking forward to reaching it. Late in the morning, he finally slid his canoe into the lake, which gave the impression of having no end because all he could see as he gazed across it was the horizon.

The journey became more manageable as he paddled up the coast toward the northeast. His schedule was determined by him. After covering several miles, establishing camp, and taking his time fishing for dinner, he could call it a day and end his journey. He also set traps for small game such as beaver, rabbits, and squirrels. The activity that brought him the most pleasure was big game hunting. The fact remains, however, that the additional effort required to transport such cumbersome kills would make his journey impossible. Therefore, he limited himself to hunting small game and searching the waters for fish.

Qaletaqa ventured to uncharted territories each day. Near the locations that would later become known as Petoskey, Harbor Springs, and Cross Village, he met members of other Anishinaabe tribes. He taught himself how to paddle while dragging bait behind his canoe, and fishing quickly became his primary focus. Waves and currents were kept to a minimum thanks to the gentle winds that swept across the water. Because of this, he could continue moving while gathering the necessary food. He thanked the Sun God daily for protecting him from the cold, keeping him dry, and making the journey pleasant and uncomplicated.

But without fail, the passage of time brings about change. After several months had passed, the evenings turned chilly, and the wind picked up a bite that punctured the animal skins he had been wearing. He knew winter was rapidly approaching and would soon be upon him. He was unconcerned because there was still a good catch to be had and a lot of good paddling in front of him.

Qaletaqa paddled further away from shore and as his paddling and fishing abilities improved, he gained more self-assurance. He could now land larger lake trout and atikameg, also known as whitefish, as he ventured out to deeper water. Atikameg were challenging to catch, but one didn't need many to make a meal. In even deeper waters, he searched for the elusive gigantic muskie. He recalled stories told by his parents and grandparents about bringing in this scrapper monster, which often took several hours to reach the boat.

Then Qaletaqa's good fortune began to change. The fierceness of the breezes was shifted to the east by the wind, and the howling of the winds increased. Residents of Qaletaqa were accustomed to the fact that strong winds would build throughout the day. However, they subsided as evening approached, making it possible for him to paddle back to shore and set up camp. On a day in October when the wind wouldn't let up and the sky was getting darker, his luck ran out. Qaletaqa was so preoccupied with reeling in bigger and bigger fish, he was oblivious to the gusts of wind pushing him to deep water. When he finally looked up and noticed the sun setting low in the western sky, he was far from shore.

Qaletaqa, realizing he was in trouble, reeled in his final line and started paddling in the direction of the tree line. He was a great distance from shore and safety. He asked himself, *Have I made a mistake?* Self-doubt was rare for the young man most comfortable in water and wilderness.

His canoe was buffeted by wind and waves. He exerted all his strength to keep the boat pointed squarely into the wind and on a strait heading to shore, to no avail. Qaletaqa's strength waning, he was unable to fight the wind and waves any longer. He carefully allowed the wind to turn his canoe away from the distant shore and safety and head into unknown deep water and a darkening horizon. With his paddle dug deep in the churning water to stabilize his canoe, he prayed to the gods to keep him safe while howling winds and white-capped waves grew in intensity.

Chapter 2
Aki

Aki was spoken of as a unique individual even by the leaders of the tribe. Her stunning appearance was hypnotic. She had a slender build with long, luxurious black hair that trailed behind her when she ran. Her body was lithe and elegant. When she fixed her gaze on you, her deep-set, midnight eyes pierced into your very being. Because of these qualities, she was the most desirable woman in the tribe that lived on the island. Their abode would eventually be known as Beaver Island, the largest island in a group of islands located thirty miles off the mainland of Michigan's northwest coast.

Every young man in the tribe tried to get her attention, even if it was only for a split second. If they were successful, the event became one that the young men would embellish for years, telling their friends and brothers about "the moment when she could have been mine."

Aki stood out from the other members of her tribe for an even more significant reason: she was the tribe's resident healer. She was blessed with the ability to diagnose and treat almost any illness that befell a member of the tribe. The tribe agreed that Aki could communicate with the Spirit world to receive guidance on healing and care for those who were ill.

Aki, however, said she learned about medicines from her mother, grandmother, and great-grandmother before them. She did not speak to Spirits. She just listened for advice from the Spirit world or, in an ethereal sense, from her departed great-grandmother, Nokomis. Aki was intuitive to the ways of healing because she had been around it all her life. She was accustomed to receiving insight from the Spirit world. Sometimes, it would just come to her as inspiration when she was unsure how to heal a fellow tribe member.

Her profile as a healer made her influential in the tribe in her own right, even though her father was Chief Decomsie, who governed as both elder and sage.

Finding different kinds of plants, roots, and herbs to use in medicine preparation for Aki's people was one of Aki's favorite activities. She would go on long, solitary treks through the woods to collect the items she needed, and she thoroughly enjoyed these outings.

The flirtatious boys and envious women in her tribe were constantly nagging her, but long hikes foraging for herbs got her away from them. They were of no assistance to her in her mission to heal others and collect medicinal remedies. She had no interest in men with narrow perspectives who wanted nothing more than to make her their wife. Nobody was interested in gaining a deeper understanding of the real her. They simply regarded her as the most valuable prize. And the young females, ugh! They were utterly insane for having the audacity to believe that she would have any interest in any of their men.

Her contemplation took place in the woods. She took her time gathering her plants, allowing herself to clear her mind of extraneous clutter and concentrate on ways to help her patients recover from their conditions. Walking along the expansive beaches of stone and sand was one of her favorite pastimes on the island. She enjoyed the forest of massive virgin hemlock pines that covered the entire island nearly as much; she could disappear amongst their majestic trunks for hours without interruption. However, she frequently fantasized about what lay beyond the vast freshwater bodies that faded into the distance beyond the horizon.

Occasionally, Aki would find artifacts from remote tribes that had washed up on the shore. She frequently questioned her sanity by pondering the origin of these items. She discovered pottery vessels with wide mouths embellished with braided and twisted cords, eating utensils, and sturdy hunting arrows.

These objects inspired her to believe there was more to this world than just her small tribe living on their isolated island. There had to be exceptional people like her who cared about other people and even new acquaintances who would value her expertise more than her physical attractiveness. She had an innate faith, the kind of faith passed down from one generation to the next, and she knew that there were people in the world like this.

This vision was ingrained in her very being, and it did not matter to her whether the people in it would be friends, comrades, or something else entirely. She could not explain how she had obtained such knowledge. She just did. Because Aki was so preoccupied with her thoughts and with searching for the medicine she needed in the forest, her acute senses failed to notice the eyes following her.

***

Onadaga was feared by his peers. He bullied the weaker and younger braves, relentlessly poking fun or laughing in the face of anyone who made a mistake. He could do it because of both size and power—he was tall, strong, and the son of Odem, the number one elder and next in line to become Chief.

Onadaga took on the same anger that exuded from his father from years of being second behind the Chief. Because of his harsh demeanor and constant lecturing, Onadaga was disliked by everyone. Despite this, everyone tolerated him and pretended to be his friend to avoid getting on his bad side. If you got on his bad side, life in the tribe could become problematic.

The fact that Chief Decomsie's daughter Aki ignored him stoked the fires of his rage even further. He believed that he was the young brave in the tribe who wielded the most influence, and as such, he deserved Aki's hand in marriage. No one else was deserving of her. There was no one else who could compete with him. However, his advances toward her were either disregarded or made fun of in front of his friends and peers. He had had enough of being made to feel ashamed.

Today things would be different.

He followed behind her into the woods, where she regularly searched for medicinal plants and herbs. He could not fathom the motivation behind her need to look after everyone else. Why couldn't she just act like a normal person and spend more time playing games and having fun with the younger members of the tribe? He did not understand why she wouldn't want to spend time with him.

Her back turned to him and her body bent at the waist, she was observing some plants with violet flowers growing close to the river.

Her body is so beautiful, her manner so delicate, he thought.

Aki heard the footfall and spun just as he grabbed her arm. She was quick on her feet, but so was Onadaga from years of hunting prowess.

"Onadaga," she said with surprise, "what are you doing out here?" She was taken aback. She didn't realize that he was following her. *Why is he here?* she asked herself.

"I wanted to talk with you alone. I plan on asking your father for your hand tonight." Onadaga stared deep into Aki's eyes. He traced a finger down her arm. "We belong together. It's time." He saw a slight smile spread on her lips as she stared at him. He thought that maybe she was happy to hear this news. Perhaps she was playing games with him, trying to make him work for her attention. As he continued to stare at her, the smile turned inwards, and she stifled a laugh.

There it was. The little laugh that made him so angry. His face turned red. *How dare she!* His grip on her arm tightened slightly.

"You don't want to marry me. We have nothing in common, Onadaga," she said. "Besides, I'm nowhere near ready for marriage and far too busy helping others who need my attention."

"Plus, you are the worst person I've ever met," Aki imagined her also saying.

Aki tried to be as polite as possible because she could sense the anger in his demeanor.

"Yes, I do want to marry you, and you will. Your father will not deny Odem's son. Our marriage will bring more stability and power to the tribe. It's meant to be," Onadaga stated sternly. He was used to getting things his way, and it infuriated him to have someone go against him.

"You think you will gain more power and favor as son-in-law to the Chief. I certainly don't see how our relationship would help the tribe. I will simply tell my father no, and he will deny your request," Aki replied. She knew how stubborn and spoiled he was, but this involved her and her future. She was going to have a say in it.

This made Onadaga angrier. He grabbed her with both hands, slipped his leg behind her, and pushed her to the ground. Aki struggled to get free, but he was a powerful young man from years of wrestling with members of the tribe. He tried to kiss her, but she was quick to avoid him.

"You will submit to me," he growled.

Aki was terrified. She had never seen him take someone on so violently. His hands held onto her, keeping her from moving off the ground. She couldn't believe that this was happening to her.

If I screamed, would anyone hear me? How far away am I from the village? she thought.

Aki tried kneeing his groin but he forced his body's weight down upon her. His legs pushed hers apart while he shoved his hand into her groin. He gave up trying to kiss her and grabbed her right breast, tearing off the cloth covering her. His excitement grew as he eyed her nakedness.

Aki screamed.

Chapter 3
Peril

As icy winds continued to batter Qaletaqa's canoe and waves grew taller and more turbulent, Qaletaqa quickly realized that he was in a dangerous situation and needed to act soon, before it was too late.

Claps of thunder could be heard coming from the clouds, which were getting darker as the storm progressed. Descendants told him that the wingbeats of animikii, also known as thunderbirds, were responsible for producing thunder. These birds also shot bolts of lightning from their claws. The mishikinebik, or water serpents, were turning the lake into roiling waves with their enormous tails. Qaletaqa could not recover from this setback due to the great distance that separated him from the coast. He was instructed to swim in the large lake while staying as close to shore as possible early in his life. He knew better than to venture this far from shore, but schools of larger fish lured him into deeper waters.

Qaletaqa concluded that he would not be able to make it back to shore. The effort of paddling against the wind and waves had worn out his arms to the point where they were useless. He had no choice but to go with the flow of the wind and current. He was in a hopeless situation. It was abundantly clear that no matter where he went, there would not be a safe landing because he had reached the point where he could no longer hold his own against mother nature. He could no longer resist her. He must let her guide him. Qaletaqa sharply turned the canoe and his broad back to the wind. After driving his paddle deep into the churning waters, he sped along with the waves as they rolled over him.

He was now totally enveloped in darkness, and the wind picked up speed. Qaletaqa could not see over the rising wave crests. He had no idea where he was or where he would end up.

As hours passed, he struggled to keep his grip on the paddle. His small canoe was propelled down the back of each aquatic arch racing faster and faster with little control. Waves twenty feet high pummeled him on the way down only to propel him back up again. Throughout the entirety of the ride, the waves reached increasingly impressive heights.

Then a new assault on his helpless vessel was formed by the convergence of three waves simultaneously. Even though he had only caught a fleeting glimpse of the water barrier out of a sliver of his eye, the enormity of this wall of water made his blood run cold. He was lifted into the air by the rogue wave until he had the impression he was standing on top of a small mountain in the middle of this enormous inland sea. Qaletaqa paddled furiously with every ounce of strength he possessed to keep his boat upright. The rogue wave sent him down its massive back, hurtling Qaletaqa toward the bottom of the wall of water. Just as he thought he was under control, he looked up to see the wave crest thirty feet above his head. Continuing to rise, it began to curl, blocking his view of the starry night sky. The wall of water came crashing down with incredible force.

Qaletaqa was able to take one final breath before the massive wave tore his canoe to shreds and threw him into ice cold water.

***

As Aki worked to free herself from the difficult situation, she moved her right arm beneath her body. Her hand brushed a fist-sized rock. Aki grabbed the rock and swung at Onadaga, delivering a direct and flush blow to the adversary's temple. Her body was flooded with adrenaline, fueling her instinct to survive and assisting her in reacting quickly to the situation. A grimace formed on his face as his eyes closed. It was a combination of expressions of surprise, disappointment, and confusion. Aki pushed his lifeless body to the side, jumped to her feet, and sprinted in the direction of the village on shaky legs. Drawing the fabric of her ravaged clothes across her breasts and draping it around her shoulders, she managed to conceal her body.

Each step that she took was accompanied by a trembling sensation on her part. She moved forward one step at a time despite the overwhelming feeling of disbelief that washed over her.

How is it possible that something of this nature took place? What was the motivation behind his behavior? The questions kept repeating in Aki's mind over and over again. She was well aware of his prowess as a hunter and combatant. Despite this, she had never in her wildest dreams considered the possibility that he would be violent toward her.

She turned her head to check if he was rushing up behind her every few moments. His stealth was incredible. He had followed her on this trip without her knowing, so she knew he could efficiently sneak up behind her. The slightest movement of bushes or leaves sent shivers down her spine.

She slowed to a walk as she got closer to the safety of her village, looked back one last time to reassure herself that she was the only one there, and then made her way to the sanctuary of her wigwam to seek refuge from the dangers that she faced. It was a stroke of good luck that none of her family members were there, including her father. She wailed into the soft comfort of the warm furs that adorned her bed until the initial shock of the assault was no longer fresh in her mind. She buried her head in the plush comfort of the furs and tried to stop shaking.

With her previous experience treating injuries, she knew that Onadaga would be unconscious for some time, but she also knew that he was not in a life-threatening condition. She would have to deal with whatever he tried next, but she was confident that her father, the Chief, would take her side and protect her if the situation became dire. Despite this, Aki believed that she must keep the attack a secret from everyone, including her father. The tribe placed a high priority on the protection and nourishment of its young warriors. Even though she was the Chief's daughter, the elders would trust Onodagas word more than hers, and the situation would escalate into a dispute that no one could win. It had the potential to cause strife within the tribe, which was something no one wanted.

She was experienced in self-defense, and the attack only strengthened her resolve to leave the isolated island and travel throughout the rest of the world. She wanted to find a place that would have a more significant impact on her life. A world that would acknowledge her abilities as a healer and allow her to help people everywhere.

She no longer wanted to worry about Onadaga. She wanted to be rid of him and never see him again.

In her hand she held a small knife that had been crafted by her father and that she usually kept by her bedside. She devised a plan to protect herself in the future by learning how to stow the knife under her clothing. She vowed that she would never again allow herself to be in such a vulnerable position and never leave her wigwam without it. She would not relax and would keep her senses on high alert, no matter where she was or what she was doing.

Chapter 4
The Light

Qaletaqa was under the impression that a brilliant moon was covering the sky above him. The light was so intense that he needed both hands to shield his eyes. As his eyes became accustomed to the brightness, he became aware that he was traveling at breakneck speed while remaining weightless and floating like he was in a lake. He was moving toward the light.

"This feels like a dream," Qaletaqa spoke aloud. "Am I dreaming?"

When one dreams in a deep sleep, their Spirit ventures upward to the sky. This was known as the sky vault, the land of enlightenment and wisdom. This is what the elders explained to him when he was a child.

Qaletaqa never really understood how this was possible. This was where Spirits resided after they departed. How was it possible for a human to be here?

Am I dead, or am I dreaming? he thought.

The last thing he remembered was being in his canoe while waves pounded him.

I must be dead. I likely drowned.

But instead of feeling helpless or suffering, he felt like a ray of sunshine blasting through time and space without a care in the world. Qaletaqa smiled.

As he took in his environment, he became aware that he was not alone. It seemed as though there was a calming presence beneath him. He discovered that he was perched atop an elk significantly more prominent than any other elk he had ever seen. The animal gave off brilliant colors of light, which appeared to be an endless array of spectral colors. These colors were more intoxicating than anything he had seen in his world.

In most cases, a person would sense the weight of an animal of this size beneath them. As they moved as one, with the glorious light trailing behind, he could sense a feeling of peace. Even though they were moving at a rapid pace, he had the impression that they were weightless. It was an amazing feeling and he didn't want it to end. He could not care less where the massive animal was taking him, but he guessed that the elk was transporting him to the great sky vault.

The elk turned its head as they floated through this otherworld, and his dark-brown eyes locked with Qaletaqa's. Qaletaqa was unable to tear his eyes away. At first, he was struck by the sense of calm that the elk's eyes gave off. However, the longer he looked, the more he realized that he was familiar with these eyes. The elk appeared to peer right through him and into his very being. There was a sharp pang of recognition there.

It turned out to be the same elk he had killed in the woods near his home. He was overcome with an intense sense of humiliation.

Qaletaqa apologized, "I'm so sorry, great elk. I'm truly sorry for taking your life."

Qaletaqa was aware of the elk's thoughts even though the animal did not communicate verbally. They had merged into one another. They had a perfect understanding of one another.

"That is not necessary," the elk said. "I was in the woods near your village so you could hunt me down. I am here to give, just like the other animals and plants. I gave myself to you so your tribe could eat for several weeks."

Qaletaqa fell silent as the elk's words struck him. Knowing that what he did was simply a part of the life cycle was humbling.

"You did supply me and my tribe with needed food for this journey," Qaletaqa said when he found his voice again.

"You will learn much on your journey. This is only the second plane of the Spiritual world you will encounter. There are seven planes of existence. There is plenty more for you to experience on this journey," the elk responded. Qaletaqa sat there confused.

"Second? I don't remember the first," Qaletaqa asked.

"You have been living in the first plane, Qaletaqa. You are now experiencing the beauty of the second." The elk turned its head back toward their flight. "Is it not something to behold?"

It was pretty extraordinary.

He thought his village's location was lovely and peaceful. The woods were densely forested with large hemlock pines, rivers and streams ran through the land with crystal-clear water, and the light-blue sky seemed to shine all the time.

Looking around him, everything had been elevated in its beauty. The trees had grown and sprouted more leaves. The pools of water were clear enough to see marine life at the bottom. The sky was bright, with a lovely light trailing behind the majestic elk he rode.

This felt like a dream, but his body seemed present. He was living this and watching scenery bloom before him.

"This is beyond words. It looks so peaceful. These are the largest trees I have ever seen. Everything is different. The colors, the grass, the water, the clouds, the sky. I have lived amongst these things and never seen them before," Qaletaqa admitted.

"Every tree and plant on the second plane are much larger and stronger because they have had the time to establish strong roots as they grow. All life should begin with deep roots. Wouldn't you agree, Qaletaqa?" the elk asked.

Qaletaqa recalled a tree in his village that was the tallest. It was allowed to develop on its own without interference from anyone, and no one was permitted to touch it. It had been there ever since the tribe first settled in this area, and it had survived even after they had cut down the rest of the trees surrounding it. To all members of the tribe, it served as a timely reminder to respect the natural world. The tree avoided falling due to the depth of its roots. It had a close relationship with the soil, supplying it with nutrients and providing shade and shelter for various minuscule animals.

"The largest trees in my forest back home are the hemlock pines. Like many other trees, they have strong roots and never blow over in a storm," Qaletaqa recalled.

"Trees, plants, flowers, weeds, and living beings should start their lives with strong roots. These roots set a solid foundation. This is what creates and nurtures the second plane. Most people learn this over many lifetimes. The second plane is also about sharing this light and knowledge with others. The light you see and how it makes the world look different will help you relax. Easing mind is what the second plane is about, settling the mind—and body—for meditation," the elk explained. Qaletaqa froze slightly.

"I have never meditated before. I find it hard to keep my mind clear," Qaletaqa admitted. He was not someone who sat around and did nothing. He was constantly running around for the tribe or with his family. He did not need anything to fall asleep as his body would be exhausted by the end of the day, and he would sleep soundly through the night.

Meditation was for those who had time and questions they needed answers to. Qaletaqa was not that kind of person.

"If you drink in the beauty of this new second plane and relax your body, close your eyes, and concentrate on the light pouring into your mind, you can meditate," the elk said. "Spirits on the second plane are here to keep an eye on their loved ones on Earth and quiet their mind in preparation for the third plane. Quieting your mind is essential for meditation."

Qaletaqa closed his eyes and concentrated on what the elk said. It was difficult because he was still processing everything that had just occurred. He was still trying to accept his death and was now being transported to the sky vault with this elk he had killed in his human form. He still had so many questions.

"The light behind us is your light. It is your Spirit and life force for eternity. This light will give you everything you need, from knowledge to energy to peace and serenity. The more you meditate, the easier it becomes to relax your mind and body. The more you relax, the closer you are to your inner Spirit," the elk said. Qaletaqa continued to concentrate, waiting to feel something. It was becoming frustrating as his mind just wouldn't turn off.

"Knowing your inner Spirit is essential for living a fulfilled life on Earth and remaining true to your Spirit throughout eternity. In fact, it is impossible to progress to more beautiful Spirit planes unless you know and respect your inner Spirit. Meditation allows you to progress through the Spirit world. Everything revolves around meditation."

Qaletaqa gave what he heard some serious thought. If what the elk said was correct, the world would be very different, and he would play a much more significant role in the world than he had ever imagined possible. If he hadn't traveled so far from home, he would never have discovered such valuable knowledge and was he supposed to share it. At the very least, he was taking in this information.

"Who enters this new world, or plane?" Qaletaqa asked. "And why?"

The elk did not hesitate to answer him. "It is the inhabitants of the second plane's responsibility to help others and themselves. Some souls are so traumatized by their Earthly experiences and reincarnation that they need time to recover. Other souls simply require a break or a vacation. This break will prepare and energize them for the next Spiritual plane.

There is far more to life than the physical plane you are familiar with on Earth. In reality, this is only the beginning."

The elk paused before saying, "You are special, Qaletaqa, and will not stay here at this point. I will leave you now because you are destined to move on and learn more about the glorious planes of the Spiritual world that surround us. Keep the light, Great One." As the elk spoke these words, he slowly disappeared.

***

Qaletaqa panicked for a moment, thinking he'd fall from the sky, but he kept moving like the elk was still with him.

Qaletaqa shuffled his shoulders and closed his eyes, loosening his muscles. This was a lot to take in, and he still had a lot of questions. The elk stressed the importance of meditation and connecting with one's inner Spirit. It was challenging to push everything out of his mind, but he had to get to the next plane. Perhaps he could speak with his ancestors and learn more about this place.

It was difficult to concentrate on just one thing. If he was dead, his poor mother would be beside herself. His tribe would comfort her, but she would be heartbroken again, just like when she lost her husband. He couldn't help but feel for her and wonder how she would take the news of his death. He still hoped this was all a dream so he wouldn't have to worry about his mother and family back home.

After a few moments, he became aware of the silence. He felt warm and a sense of flying fast through bright light. Qaletaqa, much to his surprise, began to relax.

If I keep going, he thought, *I will end up where I belong.*

He was still unsure if he was dead or dreaming, but he hoped he would soon find out.

Chapter 5
Furious

Onadaga woke in a fog. He tried to raise himself but was unsuccessful. The relentless pounding in his head drove him back to his knees in the cool dirt. He came to the conclusion that he should not proceed too quickly. The part of his head that hurt was rubbed by the large hand that he was using. He was momentarily taken aback when he observed sticky bright-red blood covering his fingers. Because he had fought for many years, he was accustomed to seeing some blood. On the other hand, the majority of the blood was usually on his opponent.

When he finally started to regain consciousness, one of the first things he recalled was Aki hitting him on the temple with a rock. This vision fanned the flames of rage that had been smoldering within him for some time. Because he could not move, he reflected on the chain of circumstances that had resulted in his current position on the ground.

He was fed up waiting for her to make a decision and had made the decision to take charge of their future. He was adamant about expressing his feelings to her and letting her know he intended to marry her. He had not prepared himself for her decision to reject him. His rage clouded his judgment, and it's possible that he went too far, but he wanted her to recognize that he was the best option for her and nothing else mattered to him.

He was entirely unprepared for her to assault him with a rock.

He mused, "She should count her blessings that no one was nearby." In a rage, he proclaimed, "No one knocks me down without paying a price."

A minuscule portion of his mind pondered the reasons behind his actions. Had he gone as far as he could? She was someone he looked up to and had strong feelings for, and he had caused her pain. Because he needed her to be confident that they would get married, he had to be more insistent with her, but it's possible that his rage got the better of him.

He forced those ideas out of his mind and continued working. What he did was appropriate, given the circumstances. The fact that she pushed back with the same intensity demonstrated that he had not yet established complete dominance over her. He was a powerful man, and that woman should have respected his authority.

Onadaga raised himself to his knees in a deliberate manner. He waited patiently until the pounding in his head subsided and he could get his feet back under him. His legs began to shake, and he felt sick as he attempted to step forward. He was brought to his knees against his will, at which point he vomited.

"Oh, Aki, I'll get my revenge on you. I'll make you beg for mercy," he spoke aloud, spitting some bile from his mouth onto the ground. He was angry and frustrated; his pain and sickness escalated his feelings.

He had planned for this to go very differently, yet here he was, stuck on the ground with vomit and blood. If anyone were to stumble upon him right now, they would look at him and think he was weak. This was inexcusable.

He wasn't a weak man.

***

After regaining his balance and feeling less queasy, he embarked on the journey back home. It took him more than an hour, but he eventually returned to his people and their camp.

He recounted to his parents and siblings the story of a glorious hunt in which he had cornered and was about to kill a giant and obstinate badger when a sudden shift in the cliff above him caused a rockslide, which resulted in a large boulder hitting him in the head. He was knocked unconscious and woke up shortly after. Because the anger in his eyes intimidated his fellow tribe members, nobody asked him about his injury when they were curious about it.

He went on to explain that the badger was the recipient of a lucky break. "The next time we see one another, however, things won't go quite as smoothly as they did this time. I will make sure that something like this never occurs again."

Onadaga's parents exchanged looks as they pondered what could have provoked their son to become so angry over a badger. Onadaga was an excellent hunter, and he had a lot of patience when it came to tracking his prey in the wilderness. He moved stealthily and quietly, barely making a sound. His aim was dead on, and he never had a single miss.

His mother assumed that he was simply self-conscious about his fall from the rockslide. She had a deep and abiding concern for him, but she would constantly reassure him that the situation was not his fault. She mused to herself, *I guess nature just is what it is sometimes.*

On the other hand, Onadaga's father was concerned that his son wasn't telling the whole truth when he answered their questions. He was aware that his son had developed feelings for the Chief's daughter. Onadaga declared that he would personally approach the Chief to request permission to wed her.

It was very clear to everyone in the village that she had no interest in having any interaction with him. Everyone kept a close eye on him to make sure he didn't say or do anything foolish while he was around her. He was starting to get the impression that Onadaga had just done something incredibly foolish.

Chapter 6
Spiritual Planes

Qaletaqa had the impression that time had stopped for him, but in reality, he was just moving through space at a faster rate. He had lost his ability to look down and take in the vastness of the planet below him. The vibrant greens, blues, and yellows had disappeared from the scene.

It was still unclear to him whether he was dreaming or dead at this point. He was still in the air, but he had the distinct impression that he was surrounded by darkness, so he questioned whether or not he had somehow made it back to the storm. He observed that the lights were still flashing by him at a faster rate now; they were white, red, and violet in color. He noticed a figure—could it have been a dog?—moving quickly to his right side.

This animal, too, shone with a brilliant light, just like the elk. When Qaletaqa turned his head to examine the creature and get a better grasp of what it was, he realized that it was not a dog. He could tell it was a wolf due to the muscular chest and the deep throat that was covered in shimmering dark-gray fur. As the beast got closer, the man's breathing became more labored, and his heartbeat became faster.

Qaletaqa slid his eyes shut in preparation for the inevitable assault as it crept closer. In the whirl of lights and endless movement, the two individuals moved around one another and circled the space between them. This was at a different time and in a different location. The control he once had in his world, where he could hunt and protect himself, was no longer available to him.

Qaletaqa slowly came to the realization that this was not simply a wolf seeking vengeance for the death of his brother; just like the elk, this was the same wolf that he had killed in the woods earlier.

Qaletaqa was concerned that this meeting would be very different from the one in which he had engaged with the elk. The elk had provided an explanation for his sacrifice, which included the reasoning behind why it was a natural process. Qaletaqa had his doubts about whether or not the wolf would have the same reaction.

The wolf had to be killed, not for its meat, but for Qaletaqa's own well-being. At this very moment, Qaletaqa was filled with nothing but regret, and if this wolf were to tear him to shreds right now, Qaletaqa would stand there and let it happen. He'd killed the wolf and brought it back to his tribe as a trophy to demonstrate his strength and prowess in front of his fellow hunters.

As the wolf's warm breath touched his neck, he closed his eyes and prepared for the agony that would come from his vengeance. But instead of anger, he experienced an overwhelming sense of righteousness.

Qaletaqa gradually opened his eyes. The enormous wolf looked him in the eyes, allowing a serenity to flow over him. His gaze was soft as if he was smiling at him.

"Greetings, Great One," the wolf said. "Are you well?"

"I…think I am," Qaletaqa replied, very unsure about himself. "Are you the same wolf I killed in the summer? I am sorry for what I did."

"I am the same wolf, Great One," the wolf replied. "You were only protecting yourself, and you did it admirably. I was only there following my purpose on the first plane."

Qaletaqa stilled for a moment as he took in those words. He was on the first plane, Earth, just like the elk had said. So these two were connected to this place?

"So, you know all about these planes as well?" Qaletaqa asked.

"Yes, I am aware of the seven planes. My Spirit has been around longer than the elk, and I have experienced a lot more through the ages," the wolf explained. "That's why I'm here to show you the third and fourth Spiritual planes."

Qaletaqa became aware that he was traveling quicker than he had with the elk. Rather than flowing with the light, he moved through it, creating his own smooth path. Large, brilliant objects were hurtling past him, or he was being hurtled past them. It was difficult to tell.

The scenery around him changed quickly. It was almost like a blur. He couldn't tell what things were or where they were.

"Where are we?" Qaletaqa asked.

"We are on our way to the third Spiritual plane," the wolf stated. "On this plane, you will feel whole in all physicality. Had you lost a leg on Earth, it would regrow here. If you had an arrow stuck in your heart, it would disappear with no residual pain."

"Oh," Qaletaqa realized. "Then this is where you were able to heal?"

"Do not worry yourself, Great One," the wolf consoled. "I finished my mission on Earth, and now I help others of all kinds, from human to animal, navigate the third Spiritual plane. That is why I was assigned to assist you."

Qaletaqa just let that sink in for a moment. Were these his Spiritual leaders? Was this a part of his Spiritual journey? Qaletaqa felt at ease, but he still felt questions racing through his mind. Why was he learning about the seven planes? What was the purpose of knowing such things?

The more he was told, the more confused he became. He wanted answers.

They arrived at a pulsing, vibrant scene that had arisen from the light. It was a plane of existence like Qaletaqa's home on Earth. The sky was bluer than he had ever seen, and even the brown dirt looked alive with possibility. People worked diligently amidst the lush colors.

"This is beautiful," Qaletaqa admitted. It was brighter and lush everywhere. He looked into the sky and noticed three glowing orbs shining brightly. "Are those all suns? It appears to be three suns, unlike the single sun we have on Earth."

"It never gets dark here on the third Spiritual plane. This way, we can work more," the wolf explained. "And with no bodily issues to worry with, we can accomplish so much more than on an Earth day."

Qaletaqa was again breathless. It was a dimension that transcended his consciousness with a welcoming, homey feel. It took him quite a while to take it all in.

Trees leafed out in vibrant hues of green, from the tropical aqua shades to the deep, earthy forest greens of the Michigan woods. The rivers ran calm, blue, and clear as any he had seen, with gentle white ripples across the tops where shiny golden rocks tipped through. Flowers and butterflies dotted the landscape in every color of the rainbow.

Animals of the woods strolled among this enchanted terrain in a leisurely manner, without concern for predators. In this world, there were none. A mountain lion walked next to a grazing deer. A brown, bushy, healthy bear slowly sauntered past rabbits and squirrels. Instead of nervously darting around, they munched on green grass or gathered stray acorns. A cougar approached Qaletaqa and brushed his arm in a show of welcome.

The light of multiple suns beamed above it all, bathing the countryside in a warm glow. The light was what brought him here and would continue to lead him.

It was becoming overwhelming for Qaletaqa. Everything was just radiant and bigger. He was surrounded by things he had never seen.

"That's the biggest river I've ever seen," Qaletaqa told the wolf. "Those trees are so big. I've never seen such vibrantly colored birds and butterflies. What else could you possibly do in a place like this? It appears to be flawless. I can't imagine there's anything else to do."

"It's not physical work," the wolf said. "It is of the Spirit. We often travel to the second plane from here to help Spirits find their way, and it takes a lot of time. We pair up with like-minded Spirits. We assist them in moving to this plane to help build our consciousness, allowing us to ascend to higher and higher planes of existence.

The wolf continued, "I'd like you to experience more of this incredible plane before we move on. Take a walk along the river, Qaletaqa. Take your time and enjoy this world for a while. When you are ready, we will move on."

Qaletaqa froze in uncertainty and fear. This plane was substantial and went on for what seemed like miles. "How will I find you? I don't know anything about this strange world or where I am," he asked with curiosity and fear. Although he was a brave man on Earth, this was all new to him, and he felt anxious about being left alone.

"You'll be just fine, and when you are ready to venture on, I will be there," the wolf reassured Qaletaqa. "Simply wander and take in everything around you."

***

Despite the solace amid this otherworldly beauty, Qaletaqa was apprehensive about being left alone in this strange, loving world. He eventually set caution aside and meandered along the river, admiring more beauty around every bend.

Qaletaqa, who was completely taken aback by the breathtaking scenery, jerked in surprise when he caught a glimpse of movement out of the corner of his eye. He appeared to be lost in thought as he cocked his head and stared. As she approached him on the other side of the river, a woman of unrivaled beauty emerged from the water that was up to her waist. The swift river presented no challenge for her diminutive but muscular frame as she navigated it with ease. She had long dark hair and eyes that looked at him with interest while she smiled warmly. Her skin was a pale caramel color, and her hair was dark.

Qaletaqa was infatuated, both Spiritually and physically. He was aware that he was looking at the woman with pure hunger in his eyes, as a young man might. But there was something else, a metaphysical link. As she approached him, it was evident she had a connection with him.

Qaletaqa took a step back, terrified by his feelings toward her. She smiled warmly and leaned in close enough for Qaletaqa to feel her body heat. He was ashamed of his desire, but she was so stunningly gorgeous and desirable—what could he do?

She approached him with the most natural movements and embraced Qaletaqa like lovers who had not seen each other in months. He returned the same embrace.

It was not a foreign feeling like he had anticipated. It felt normal and comfortable. He felt like he'd known her forever, and they'd finally come together after many years of separation. There was no need for either of them to say anything. Qaletaqa felt perfect comfort, joy, and love in this deep, gentle hug. They eventually parted ways, holding hands and facing each other.

Qaletaqa looked at her and used his voice as opposed to speaking telepathically as he had with the elk and wolf. "Who are you? I feel like I have loved you forever," he admitted.

"You have," she replied. "Qaletaqa, we've been in love for thousands of years. You don't remember since you're on another earthly adventure and haven't found me yet. You will, however. I believe in you."

Qaletaqa believed her claims to be valid. They had a magnetic draw to one another and always found each other in each generation. But how was he expected to track her down? How would they locate each other if he was here and she was on Earth? Did they lose this opportunity?

"How will I find you on Earth if you are here?" Qaletaqa questioned.

She laughed softly, still holding onto Qaletaqa's hands. "My light energy is here at the moment. Our light returns each night to re-energize for another day on Earth. Since I'm here with you, I must be sound asleep on Earth. Our light energy can do that sort of thing. Like being in two places at once." She smiled so brightly at him like he was the air she needed to breathe.

Qaletaqa considered what she was saying. In context with his otherworldly journey, it made perfect sense. So he wasn't dead; he was dreaming.

"We all return to Earth over and over and over again to experience more adventures to improve ourselves," she continued. "This is how we get to higher Spiritual planes. Every time we come back to Earth, we do so to live a different life and learn lessons from it. Each lesson helps us get ready to move to a different Spiritual plane."

Qaletaqa was beginning to understand everything that she was explaining. "So, I've been here and returned to Earth numerous times?" he asked.

"You have. In fact, you have already been to higher planes than this," she replied. "You have had so many life adventures that you may never have to return to Earth once your current Earth body dies. We are both on a higher plane. I came to see and comfort you because I have been missing you terribly."

He could feel the love radiate as she admitted her feelings to him. Through their joined hands, he could feel their Spirits become one. The thousands of years that they had been together had solidified their relationship.

"Walk with me," she told him. They walked together along the riverbanks. He felt so at ease with this woman. It felt almost too good to be true. The riverbanks with naturally trimmed paths lined with brilliant foliage seemed the perfect backdrop as he spent time with his soulmate. It seemed like it could have been hours or even days, as far as Qaletaqa could tell. The quiet peace felt like it would last forever, and he would be fine if it did.

They didn't need to say much to one another; they just walked in silence. There was no need for words when your

Spirits knew each other so well. He felt at peace with her until they were gently interrupted.

"We need to move on to the fourth plane," he heard a voice behind him say.

More work, he remembered. He turned to find the wolf, who was following behind him.

"I kind of like it here. I'd like to stay a little longer if I could."

The wolf smiled. He'd heard this before. "I don't mind, but it's not up to me."

"Well, maybe I should talk to who it is up to," Qaletaqa began, but as he turned, the woman vanished in a beam of light.

"What happened?" he said, irritated. "Where did she go? I want to follow her!"

"Soon, Qaletaqa. Very soon," the wolf reassured him. "But for now, we must move on. But remember this light. This beauty is only possible because of this light."

Remember this light? What was the wolf talking about? Qaletaqa was very confused by this. The light that the woman left in? The light that was in this plane? What was on the next plane? Was it filled with darkness or evil?

***

Before Qaletaqa could ask the wolf, he was buzzing through space again, weightless and aware of movement as he hurtled through tunnels of light.

Moving past clusters of stars, he closed his eyes, allowing his consciousness to keep up with his traveling speed. He allowed his mind to empty, and he could feel his body as it traveled. When he opened his eyes, the wolf was still next to him. They were standing on the edge of a lake surrounded by tall conifers that reached toward a bright blue sky. Dazzling white sand cascaded down to gently lapping waves at his feet.

"How are you feeling, Great One?" the wolf asked.

"Confused," Qaletaqa admitted. But there was another feeling, something new that he hadn't felt yet. It was a boundless love for the world. It was a welcome sentiment that he hoped he could take with him everywhere.

It was as if the wolf could read his thoughts.

"What you are feeling is love. Love is the focus of the fourth Spiritual dimension," the wolf began to explain. "This plane will help you understand truth and love so that planes five and six will be easier. Qaletaqa, you need to remember this. You must always have truth and love with you because that's the only way to get through the many levels of the fourth plane and move on to the next." The wolf paused momentarily. "I am going to leave you now, but don't worry, your next Spiritual guide will take good care of you. So, keep love flowing and keep the light at all costs."

Chapter 7
Follow Your Heart

The wolf began to disappear as light shot out from where it had been standing. Qaletaqa didn't feel alone without him; he felt a lot of emotions, but none were loneliness. He had gone through a lot on the third plane and felt like his brain was about to explode with all this new information.

Even though Okemos was unaware of her name, he had the utmost admiration and affection for the lovely woman he had met. Simply taking her hand was enough to fulfill his needs and he experienced an overwhelming sense of contentment knowing that she was close by.

The thought of losing her once more caused discomfort in his chest. After he watched her leave without a proper farewell, he swore to himself that he would never allow something similar to happen again. He was aware that he had to keep moving forward with this journey, but he secretly wished he could savor certain moments for much longer.

"Keep the light at all costs" were the final words spoken by the wolf. What did he mean by that? Was it the torch of this journey that needed to be kept lit so that he would remember what he was doing? What did the light represent? Passion? Love? Respect? Curiosity?

Perhaps the following Spiritual guide would be able to shed more light on this.

When a black bear emerged from the nearby woods, Qaletaqa wasn't startled at all. The bear was only five feet away from him. It did not come as a surprise to him anymore because he had become accustomed to wild animals appearing along the path he was traveling to guide him.

Before making a snap choice, Qaletaqa would always look into the eyes of the animal first. Qaletaqa felt more at ease after he saw that the eyes of the burly bear were canine-like, meaning they were soft and gentle. He recalled the final words of guidance given to him by the wolf and made sure to keep love in his heart.

The bear made its way over to Qaletaqa and sat down next to him as if the two of them had known each other for a long time. Qaletaqa was dwarfed by the size of the bear, which stood six feet tall at the shoulders and had paws that were as big as his head.

"Welcome," the bear said.

Qaletaqa started to instinctually back away but then remembered that the bear was not there to harm him but to help him on his journey. Growing up, he had been taught to respect animals and give them space. You never knew when one would hurt you. That instinct was still present, but he knew he needed to push it down during this time.

"Do you know where you are, Great One?" the bear asked.

Before he answered the question, Qaletaqa responded with his own query.

"Why does everyone keep calling me Great One?" he asked.

"Because you are," the bear answered simply.

That simply cannot be true, Qaletaqa thought to himself. He was eighteen years old but young compared to the other members of his tribe. Yes, he was a great huntsman and warrior, but he had not won any battles. He had not proven himself to his tribe just yet. No, these animals must be mistaken. His father was a Great One. He had proven himself, time and time again, to the elders and the tribe. Qaletaqa was nothing yet compared to his father. It had been years since his death, and the other villagers talked about that man like he was still alive.

Qaletaqa could only hold out the hope that he would become the kind of man his father had been. Qaletaqa would not think of himself as a Great One until he had reached the point where he could confidently say that he had followed in his father's footsteps.

Thinking about his father, Qaletaqa simply replied to the black bear, "I'm just Qaletaqa. A simple warrior on Earth. There is nothing great about me."

The bear gave off a small laugh telepathically. "In the Spirit world you are When you are not on Earth, you reside on one of the highest planes in the Spirit world. Do you know where you are now?" it asked.

"According to the wolf, I'm in the fourth Spiritual plane, heading for the fifth Spiritual plane, which I assume you are here to guide me to," Qaletaqa replied.

"Yes. In a way." The bear paused. "But it's all up to you. If you feel you can continue with this journey, then we will help you."

Qaletaqa didn't hesitate to answer the bear. "I'd like to. Every dimension is more beautiful than the next. Does that continue?"

"More beautiful and even brighter," the bear explained. "I say that because the fifth dimension is all light. There is no more form like you see here."

"Then yes. I wish to continue," Qaletaqa responded. The bear nodded in understanding but became more serious.

"Before you can move ahead, there are things you need to understand about this dimension," the bear told him.

"The journey so far has been enlightening. I'm honored to have you as a guide for this part of the journey. I don't think we've met before, but you seem as familiar to me as the elk and wolf I met on Earth, and I feel terrible that I put both of them here. But I never killed a bear like you. I'd remember something like that." Qaletaqa spoke with love and from the heart. Each of these Spiritual guides had been a memory to him, so he felt like the bear should be no different.

"We have met, Qaletaqa, but it was a long time ago in a different dimension, in a past life," the bear explained. "Our paths have often crossed as we have grown together through time. But most important is where we are now and how much truth and love you can keep in your heart."

"I was told to keep feeling love to continue my journey, so that's what I plan to do," Qaletaqa stated. He paid attention to what was being said to him and made sure to keep those words in mind throughout this whole ordeal. He was starting to get a better understanding of this journey, and he realized that the elders had been right.

"Good. Just know that sometimes you will find that to be difficult," the bear warned him. Qaletaqa realized this animal was a little more serious than the last two. His words brought warning and fear. Qaletaqa was aware that the subsequent planes would be distinct from one another, but he did not anticipate that they would be particularly difficult. However, he had faith in himself and in everything that he had achieved throughout his life.

"I think I'm quite capable. My mother taught me from a young age to be truthful in life, to myself and to everyone around me. I'm strong in most aspects of my life, so I think I can maintain a strong heart full of truth and love," Qaletaqa admitted.

"What does your heart tell you while on Earth?" the bear asked.

Qaletaqa pondered this. People had told him he was a courageous man. But what does that mean in the Spiritual world?

"My heart tells me to care for my family and hunt for food to feed my tribe. I like to hunt, and I'm pretty good at it. I am strong and can protect myself and my loved ones. But I never knew there was so much more to life other than just what there is on Earth. I think I need to rethink what's important."

Qaletaqa spoke softly as he formed his words. "Certainly, someone has to hunt and care for the tribe and my family, but there are others that could help. With my knowledge, I realize that everyone must know how much more there is to life. Am I destined to share this information with everyone?"

"That is for you to decide, Qaletaqa. Our heart is what we must listen to, as it is the instrument the Great Spirit gave us for guidance in life. Do you remember the stories about your father and the hunting expedition he never returned from?" the bear asked.

"I was too young to remember his disappearance. But I've overheard the stories. No one has been willing to tell me the story of the great hunt and the bear that attacked, and...." He went silent. "Are you that bear?"

"Your father and I have crossed paths many times, Qaletaqa. You see, we are all connected from one life to another and help each other continue on a greater journey than Earth itself." The bear paused before admitting, "Yes. I killed your father. Like you recently had to defend yourself against the wolf. It was destined that only one of us would survive in the woods that day."

Qaletaqa's body sagged as his thoughts raced to process all of this information, which left his emotions muddled. Naturally, he felt anger rising up inside of him, but he found the strength to push it aside. He had been instructed to keep that love in his heart, and this was the first test of his ability to do so. The test had arrived so suddenly. He had a limited relationship with his father, but he was able to conjure up images of him and feel love for him. He was aware that in a previous incarnation, this bear had taken his father away from him. However, that was a different life, lived on a different plane.

The black bear kept casting anxious glances in Qaletaqa's direction. The bear was inquiring as to the well-being of the young man, and Qaletaqa was attempting to assess whether or not he was. It turned out that the bear wasn't joking when he said that things were going to get more difficult. For a first test, this was a wealth of knowledge to take in.

"I'm okay," he finally managed. "I'm glad I finally know that the stories were real and that my father was a great hunter like me. Thank you for being truthful with me. He must have had a lot of courage to face a bear as big and strong as you."

"Yes, he was, Qaletaqa. But we have fun joking about it today because he has gotten the best of me in other lives," the bear laughed.

"Wait. You've seen my dad. He's here somewhere?" Qaletaqa looked around them, waiting impatiently to see his father step out from the woods somewhere. He had silently hoped that maybe he would see him here. Could this be happening now?

"He's waiting for you, Qaletaqa. He needed to know how well you could handle love through adversity. You were right. You are as strong with love in your heart on this plane as you are physically on Earth. We are all very proud of you. And don't forget, Qaletaqa, keep the light."

With that, the bear faded right before his eyes.

***

"But what do I do now?" Qaletaqa said into the now-empty space. He was confused and looked around himself briefly before the world swirled into an open space, a void of brilliance as Qaletaqa himself became the light.

He was on his way to the fifth plane, and he was aware that in order to proceed to the next step, he would need to keep his lessons in mind. It was difficult to envision what the situation could involve next.

Qaletaqa perceived a new Spirit fusing with him as a traveling companion during the subsequent leg of the journey, and the light that he was emitting was incredible and warm. They traveled through the light together, passing through stars and tunnels. While they were traveling to the next Spiritual plane, brilliant galaxies passed them by.

They traveled through regions that were filled with galaxies and constellations that featured groups of stars. After that, they separated into single, bright beacons, and then they regrouped into clusters of light. Each galaxy was enveloped in a dazzling white light that was more iridescent than the dazzling shine that it radiated. A lustrous glow emanating from beyond all the galaxies encircled everything with brilliant rays of light from a distant, unseen source. The only possible explanation for this phenomenon is that it originated on another plane of existence.

It did not matter to Qaletaqa where they went as he began to realize who had joined him at the start of this leg of the journey. This Spirit felt so connected to him that, at first, he thought it was the young woman he had met before. But this feeling was even more profound. This Spirit had a life intertwined with his. Memories filled Qaletaqa's mind as visions of happier times became known. That feeling of love and light grew stronger the longer they were together. It brought tears to Qaletaqa's eyes.

The Spirit with him was his father.

Chapter 8

The Final Planes of Existence

As they stopped, their bodies took on the silhouettes of their human bodies. As Qaletaqa looked over the man who had been gone for so many years, he could still see every detail of the stout, handsome warrior he was on Earth.

"Father, I've missed you so much," Qaletaqa said. He could feel the sting in the corner of his eyes, and tears threatened to fall.

"Son, it is so good to see you," his father said calmly.

The two men embraced one another. Qaletaqa recalled his father giving him the same comforting embrace every time he got home from a day of hunting. It was a hug that enveloped him completely. The same wave of relief that washed over him whenever his father came back to their home washed over him now as well. Even though Qaletaqa knew that this situation would only last for a short while, he welcomed it with open arms.

"I wish I could have spent more time with you on Earth," Qaletaqa admitted, still holding onto his father. "It's been so hard without you, and I always wished you could have seen more of my life."

"You didn't know it, but I've been with you every step of the way." His father pulled back, still holding onto his son's shoulders. "I was there with you in the woods on your last hunt, helping you aim your bow. I was there when the wolf attacked. I helped you stay calm and helped your arrow fly true. I was with you on the canoe that overturned and plunged you into the cold water. I have always been there with you."

"I wish I could have seen you, talked with you, hugged you, and loved you." Qaletaqa sobbed. It had been hard to lose his father at such a young age. At times in his life, he could have used him for guidance and advice. He felt like the entire village knew his father better than he ever did.

"I could always feel your love, Qaletaqa." His father pulled him back into a hug. It was for reassurance from his words and because they both knew that this time was short. "It has been strong over the years as you have grown. I have loved you just as much. I know it's difficult feeling my love for you. Open your heart as you did on the fourth plane and let love flow."

Opening his heart was not difficult in the glow of his father's Spirit. As Qaletaqa relaxed and took a deep breath, he could feel his shoulders drop. He could feel his heart open, allowing his father's love to rush in. *In my entire life, I have never felt such loving, calm contentment,* he thought. This moment was something that he had missed. It was that feeling of being loved. Yes, his mother was protective of him and showered him with her love, but a father's love was just as important as a mother's.

"I love you, Father," Qaletaqa spoke, his head buried into his father's chest. They were almost the same height, but Qaletaqa wanted to feel like that little boy again. The one that could be enveloped entirely in his father's arms.

"As I love you," his father replied. He pulled away from Qaletaqa again and allowed them some space. He wanted to look his son in the eye as they spoke again. "Love is what makes all of us. Love surrounds us. Love is more important than anything because with love filling your heart, there is no room for anything else."

"It is a wonderful feeling. So much love everywhere. I had no idea I could feel this way. Would I be able to feel this overwhelming love on Earth, Father?" Qaletaqa asked.

His father nodded, "Yes, but it requires a great deal of practice and patience. And it all begins with the truth." He held his hand to his chest, "You see, you must first emit truth from your heart and Spirit. The beginning of love is truth. Love will come if you are honest with yourself and others. It is difficult to deceive yourself or others while radiating genuine love. Some people are born with the ability to love, a remnant of their prior existence. Others must work on it. Their Spirit may have returned to Earth to do this."

"I've always been truthful. I've never had a reason to lie about anything. I have lived my life with honesty," replied Qaletaqa.

"That's good, Qaletaqa." His father patted his son's shoulder. "This fifth plane is all about truth. Not just telling the truth but living the truth every day. If you're not true to yourself, you can't be true to the rest of humanity. Some people don't know they are living a lie. They just keep living without thinking about their mission in life." He paused briefly, gathering his thoughts. "Truth is a compelling thing. You are more powerful when you follow your life path and always share the truth with others. You can accomplish more in a day than most people can accomplish in a lifetime. Living a truthful life allows you to accomplish great things, and you never have to look over your shoulder."

Qaletaqa looked at the light that was his father. He nodded to him in understanding.

"Qaletaqa, I believe you're well on your way. Bring more light into your life daily. When your mind is peaceful, patiently focus on the light. The truth is always revealed. You will be enveloped in the warmth of love. It is enough love to transform your reality altogether. Many Spirits from many realms of existence have sent you love. All from quietly concentrating on the light. The same light that you can see and feel right now.

Qaletaqa considered and absorbed what he was learning all at once. He felt it was easier to take in his father's teachings than the teachings of the animals that helped him along the way. There was nothing wrong with how they spoke to him. He just felt the comfort of his father on this plane.

"So, this is the fifth plane?" Qaletaqa asked.

"Yes. We are in the fifth plane of Spirit, which is made exclusively of light," his father replied. "That's why we are all light in this fifth Spiritual plane."

"I was told there were two more Spiritual planes after this. Will you be taking me to them, Father?"

"This fifth plane is as far as I can help you because it's all I have learned on my Spiritual journey," he admitted. "You have learned much more than I have because you have experienced more lives than I have. You are a special Spirit, Qaletaqa. It does not matter that I was your father on Earth. You may think I have more knowledge of the Spirit world than you, but it's the other way around. You are on a special path, Qaletaqa. You will come to understand this soon. I can only help you here."

Qaletaqa understood why his father would not continue on this journey with him. This surprised him, for, on Earth, he would have missed him. Instead, he was grateful for the moment spent with his father.

His father continued, "The light from the fifth plane is a source of energy for you to tap into whenever you feel the need. This is the source of all light and energy. Even from Earth, you visit here every night in your dreamless sleep to replenish your energy for another day. The more energy you expend on the world, the more we give you. So, use as much light energy as you like, Qaletaqa. The more energy you share, the more you acquire. If you want more energy, give more energy. If you want more love, give more love. The more you give of anything, the more you receive. Use the light, Qaletaqa."

Qaletaqa and his father took a leisurely stroll alongside one another, taking pleasure in each other's company. It wasn't walking so much as it was just moving together effortlessly while taking in the expansive views of the cosmos and the brilliant light that was present everywhere. The ease and comfort that they found in their love for one another were remarkable. He had high hopes that this walk would go on forever, but he was also aware that he had come to this place to gain knowledge and that he would eventually have to move on. Thinking about the energy of light, Qaletaqa did not witness the physical disappearance of his father; however, he could sense the transition of his father's energy.

It's okay, he thought. *I know I can call on my father's energy anytime I need. I can still feel you, Father. Thank you for your guidance. I love you.*

***

This experience gave Qaletaqa the closure he had always wanted with his father. As a young man he wanted to tell his father he loved him or hug him. He never got that chance. His father's departure was heartbreaking to him and his family.

Right now, he felt like he had that chance to tell his father he loved him and give him a hug. In addition, he was reassured that his father would continue to watch over him throughout his life, both on Earth and in the Spirit world, which made him feel better about and know that this was not their ending. They would have other moments just like this one again at some point in the future.

While he was moving through the light of the fifth plane, he became aware of another light moving in his direction. Qaletaqa was surprised to find that the light was brighter and warmer than it had been when he was with his father, but it had nonetheless changed. During the time that he was being bathed in a calming light, he became aware of the presence of a second figure that was either standing next to him or embracing him. He had no idea who or what it was; he could only tell that it was love.

"How are you, Qaletaqa?" the light said.

"I feel warm and loved being here with you, and I'm sorry, I don't even know who you are."

"That is quite alright, Qaletaqa. My previous Earth experience was at a different time and place from yours. I taught love then and continue to teach and live love now," the man explained. "On Earth, they called me Jesus."

He continued, "We have often met in the Spirit world, but you won't remember that while you're in an Earth experience. You are a great Spirit, Qaletaqa, destined to help change humanity for the better. Love is all you need, and I am here to help with that and show you the sixth plane. The Spiritual plane of pure love."

Qaletaqa took a deep breath and felt the intensity of love surrounding him. It was a thickness in the air as he breathed. It was a pressure his whole body felt. "I think I can feel it. It's nice here and so comfortable. I feel like I'm floating in a hot spring bath, like those that flow from a mountain," Qaletaqa replied with his eyes closed. He wanted to feel everything.

"I'm glad you like it here, because I may need your help shortly," Jesus stated.

Qaletaqa opened his eyes and looked toward the lighted silhouette. Why would this being need his help? So far, he had had numerous Spirits to guide him through the planes. He was the student, not the teacher. He learned so much that it was hard for him to think of himself as an expert on any of this.

"Why would you need my help?" Qaletaqa asked. His chest became tighter as confusion and anxiety started to creep in. This man taught pure love, and he was asking for Qaletaqa's help.

Jesus smiled at Qaletaqa as he explained. "The sixth plane is similar to the fifth plane, but rather than light, it is all thought and pure love. Everyone and everything is made up of thought. Pure thought yields pure love as well. You learned to keep love in your heart no matter what the circumstance. I need you to continue sharing that love on Earth and teaching others to exude love.

"You see, Qaletaqa, there is nothing more important than love," Jesus spoke lightly. "Love brings peace. Love brings happiness. Love can change the world. I teach love from this Spiritual plane to all. Love is all that is needed. You are a great Spirit, Qaletaqa. If you can share, teach, and be loved on Earth, you will be helping me spread my message."

Qaletaqa pondered what Jesus was telling him. He needed to do right and share his teachings of love and light with those on Earth. It was a daunting task, but maybe this was his true purpose for this journey. He had no idea how to begin or how he could educate the people around him. Still, he knew the Spirits he had spoken to would continue to guide him on this new mission.

"I will do my best to help share the message of love on Earth. It would be an honor to help you on this Spiritual plane," Qaletaqa agreed. He hesitated before admitting, "The only problem I see is that I don't know how to get back to Earth."

"Do not worry," Jesus reassured him. "When the time is right, that will take care of itself. But first, you need to see what pure consciousness is like. It is the seventh and final plane of existence."

Jesus opened his hands toward Qaletaqa. Although he slightly hesitated, Qaletaqa put his hand into the outstretched hands. Energy pulsed into Qaletaqa like lightning bolts coursing across a stormy sky.

***

He felt his body of light change into nothingness. He was still whole, but there was nothing to see or feel. He was pure thought.

Into this realm, he was welcomed with a gentle greeting. The voice came from nowhere but surrounded him. It was soft yet forceful. It was a voice of peace and calm and energy.

"Hello, Qaletaqa," the voice echoed. "I am Buddha. I deliver pure thought."

Qaletaqa stirred slightly, overwhelmed. This powerful voice frightened him as he couldn't tell where the noise was coming from. As Jesus had explained to him, this was pure consciousness. There was nothing solid here, just thought.

"It is understandable that you are confused." Buddha laughed. "This is the seventh plane, which all Spiritual beings strive to achieve. It is the plane of pure thought, or the source.

Some refer to it as God. To enter this plane, you need to be God-like. Act like God, think like God, and be like God.

Qaletaqa didn't understand. How was someone like him able to be on this plane? How was he worthy to stand in a place such as this? This is where the gods resided.

"Great Spirits you don't know yet reside in the seventh plane. Some have been on Earth, and some have yet to show up. In time, the world will learn about Spirits like myself, Mohammed, and others. But when needed, we return in one form or another," Buddha explained.

"Why am I here?" Qaletaqa asked.

"You are a great Spirit, Qaletaqa. Maybe you are not God-like yet, but you are on your way. We wanted to show you all the planes of existence and all the possibilities that lie within them. I foresee you being here as one of us someday, but you still have much to accomplish during your Earth adventure." Buddha's voice resonated around Qaletaqa. "It is time for you to return to Earth now."

***

He didn't feel himself returning through infinite galaxies of light. He felt love and warmth and a new focus toward sharing as much of this beautiful place as he could with everyone he knew.

He wished that this sensation could last for the rest of his life, but it was not meant to be. Suddenly, he felt a chill that went all the way down to his bones spread throughout his entire body. His entire being, even his heart, seemed to be made of ice.

Qaletaqa was startled out of his peaceful state of sleep, and even though the summer sun was shining from above, he was chilled to the bone. When he opened his eyes, the discomfort of the outside world that he had experienced prior to departing came flooding back to him. It hurt his head. The water and the chill that enveloped him caused his entire body to ache. At least he had confirmation that he was still alive, even though he would have much rather remained with the Spirits.

As waves of chilly water washed over his prone body, he rested on a lakeshore he didn't recognize. His furs, which ordinarily kept him warm, had been ripped from him. *What happened to the warm light?* he wondered. *Why couldn't I have stayed there? Wherever there was.*

Qaletaqa concentrated on the words from his father and the meaning of his message.

I have been given a powerful gift to share, he thought. *My Spirits believe in me sharing this gift with everyone. This is what I will do. This is why I am here. This is my gift to the world. This is my Spirit gift.*

His mind was filled with images of him instructing members of the tribe of varying ages. He could see that everyone was responding positively to his message. His travels were not yet finished.

His mind was overcome with images originating from the Spirit world. The lessons he had learned there came flooding back to him in clear detail. Qaletaqa had received a significant amount of education, and with the assistance of the light, he was finally starting to comprehend the material. His discoveries from the spirit world and truths that were shared had the potential to help all people lead happier lives while on Earth. There are some facts that absolutely have to be made known to everyone.

Qaletaqa knew he needed to share everything with tribes like his own so that everyone could benefit from what he now understood. But how could he help them realize just how important this information was? And how would he share it?

He understood most of the truths, and now, as an earthly emissary, he had to determine how to inform others. He needed to focus on key areas and compile them into a list. This was a lot to take on, and he wondered what the most crucial elements were?

The light, he thought. *The importance of the light is what they need to understand. They need to know that they can access this light so easily through quiet reflection in their* mind. *Through a calm mind, they will learn the truths of the Spirit world through Spirit itself.*

Qaletaqa concentrated on these truths and organized them in his mind.

Eleven. Yes, eleven. I will share eleven truths that all tribesmen can live by. Eleven truths from the Spirit world that will allow everyone to live in perfect harmony.

Qaletaqa laboriously dragged himself up the dune, pausing periodically to catch his breath and give the throbbing in his back time to lessen in intensity. The light began to warm and heal him as he made his way up the dune, using one arm to pull himself up and the other to push himself forward. He succumbed to exhaustion and fell asleep.

***

When he came to, he discovered that he was sleeping in a wigwam that was very much like the one that served as his home. He was warmly wrapped in animal skins. His entire body continued to hurt.

He wondered if this place was real or if his body would vaporize into bright light, and he would travel through the stars once more as the animal skin warmed his tired muscles. There was a sliver of him that secretly wished he could have continued his life in that place. The love that he experienced there was incomparably superior to the love that he could ever hope to experience here. He was aware that he had returned to Earth because both Jesus and Buddha had informed him that he would one day do so.

Qalatqa propped himself up on one elbow as his thoughts tried to piece together where he was and what had happened. Before the thought could form, gentle hands and the smiling face of a woman appeared from above him and encouraged him to return to the lying position. Although he had never seen her before, he found that her presence was very calming. The reassuring grin that his benefactor wore gave him confidence.

He began to drift back into unconsciousness, a fading thought of her eyes remaining in his mind.

96

Chapter 9
Returning

A local hunting party came across the young man on the beach where they lived and found him unconscious, drenched in water and cold. Soon after, word spread amongst the tribe about the strange young man from a distant land who had mysteriously washed up on their shore.

The medicine woman of the tribe, Aki, was in charge of providing care for the warrior and seeing to it that he made it through the ordeal alive. The fact that he was drenched and cold led her to believe that he had been in the water and had been washed up on shore. Because there was no trace of a boat or any of his belongings, it was unclear whether he was traveling with a group or by himself.

The elders of the tribe and the Chief were eager to sit down with the outsider in order to learn more about his background and how he had arrived at their location. Aki made an effort to keep them at bay until she was certain that he had

had enough time to recover and strength to withstand their interrogation. He wasn't even conscious, much less able to communicate in any way. She was successful in rousing him from his sleep long enough for him to take a few sips of water and broth. On the second day, he gradually gained more consciousness, putting an end to her fears that he would not make it through the first round of treatment.

Aki was mixing a salve for a fellow tribe member when she heard the man start to mutter. She turned to him and watched as he pushed himself up slightly. She sat on the bed next to him and watched his movements.

He mumbled some words in a language that wasn't her tribe's, but since they were similar to the language that her people spoke, she thought he was asking where he was. Because she was concerned that they wouldn't be able to have a conversation with each other, she reached out and touched his hand before telling him, "You are safe."

She grabbed a water bowl beside the bed and offered it to him. He tried to capture the bowl from her, but she calmly said, "Let me help you." He gave a small smile from the corner of his mouth in understanding.

She made the bowl available to him by positioning it in close proximity to his mouth as she spoke. This was the most water he had consumed in the previous few days, and he drank it in a few gulps this time. If she hadn't stopped him, he would have consumed it all with an insatiable thirst.

"Go slow. It would be best if you didn't get sick," she warned him. He lay back and closed his eyes for a moment. She thought he would fall asleep until he slowly opened them again and stared at her.

"What is your name?" he asked.

It took her a moment to understand what he asked, but she smiled and replied, "Aki. What is your name?"

"Qaletaqa." There was relief on his face as he said his name. She was glad to see him relax back into bed. She offered the water to him again, reminding him to take it slow. She could tell he was getting tired again and said to him that resting was okay. She would remain here. He took her words in and gave another smile. His eyes closed, and he let sleep take over again.

The elders of the tribe were adamant about having a conversation with the young man. Aki was able to communicate his name and the fact that their language was modified slightly from his own. They had high hopes that since Aki could comprehend what he was saying, it wouldn't be too difficult for them to acquire additional information about him.

After several days of persistent urging, Aki gave in to the elders' demands and agreed to let them bring the stranger some much-needed food. It was a gesture of goodwill so that they could start questioning their guest, and the food provided would hopefully show that.

***

Qaletaqa was taken aback by the fact that he was able to comprehend the questions they were asking him. The dialect was not the same as the one spoken by his tribe, but it was close enough for him to understand. It was peculiar to see other people. Even though he was aware of the existence of other communities, he felt as though he was experiencing something entirely new in this very place and time.

They started off by asking him straightforward questions. His name, as well as the place where he was from. They were perplexed as to why he had gone to such great lengths to get there and were surprised to find him lying on a beach. They were surprised when they learned that he had traveled a long distance away from his family.

Qaletaqa shared the story of his adventure that took him from his tribe to the great lake and into the storm that destroyed his canoe with a heavy wave. From there, he had no recollection.

He described his journey into the seven planes. He talked about traveling through the warm light above the stars and meeting with Spirits who guided him. It sounded unbelievable to the elders.

"What did these Spirits look like?" Chief Decomsie asked.

"Like animals here on our lands. I met with great Spirits that looked like an elk, a wolf, and a bear. But they were made of bright light. They showed me many beautiful things and dimensions of our world that I didn't know existed."

"Could they speak?" asked an elder.

"Why, yes, sort of. At least, I knew exactly what they were thinking. And they knew exactly what I was thinking. We weren't talking, though."

"What did they share with you," another elder asked.

Qaletaqa pondered this question, which he had asked himself a few times. It had seemed like an eternity while he was there. He thought about everything he had been through, the Spirits that shared their knowledge, and his father. He had spoken with his father and learned so much in so little time.

His heart felt like it was beating in his chest when he realized he had accomplished his mission. His future lay in what he learned and sharing it with other people. He had found his purpose, his gift.

His eyes brightened.

"I learned that there is so much beyond our life here on Earth. There are many worlds even more beautiful than what you see around you. Some are similar to here but with vibrant colors that take your breath away. Others are made of just light. Brilliant light but soft to the eye and peaceful." Qaletaqa described the planes the best that he could. "I was taught many lessons by the Spiritual guides. They spoke about how these ideas need to be shared with others. I believe I've been given a gift." Qaletaqa had finally said the words aloud. He had been given his Spirit Gift.

As the Chippewa elders took in his tale, they spoke in murmurs, punctuating their points and questions with excited hand gestures pointing to the heavens.

Chief Decomsie calmed the others down and looked dubiously at Qaletaqa. "A gift? What is this gift you talk of?"

"The gift of sharing. I learned that there is so much more," Qaletaqa explained. "The Spirits that you worship are there. They have shown me how special life is. And not just here, but when you leave here. The great Spirits taught me so much, but most importantly, I think they wanted me to share my experience with you."

He looked at the faces of the elders, who watched him blankly. He could only hope they understood.

"There is so much more to life than what you see around you," Qaletaqa continued. "So much more than your tribe, this hunting country, and the magnificent lakes you have visited. Examine the night sky. Beyond all those stars, a completely new planet begins. Our ancestors are there to look after us after we leave this planet. Then there are other realms beyond that." Qaletaqa rambled on and on.

While explaining his journey to the tribe elders, he realized he had so much to share. Everyone should know about the strange and beautiful worlds beyond the stars.

The Chief and all the elders saw Qaletaqa transform as his eyes deepened and he beamed. They could not look away from him. They were watching a true believer.

The excitement, the knowledge, and his conviction kept them at ease. Qaletaqa transfixed them. Was it possible this young warrior was sent to them by the Spirits they worshipped?

The elders wanted to fill themselves with his knowledge. They all started asking questions at once. Aki saw this happening and stepped in to stop them.

"Our guest must rest," she said. "Please, Father. These questions can wait another day."

"You are right, my dear. Let us allow our special guest to rest," Chief Decomsie replied.

With that, the elders and the Chief departed.

As Aki attended to Qaletaqa, he relaxed and let all his new realizations sink into his conscious mind. But was it all real, or did he have a vivid dream? It was all genuine to him, but he wondered if everyone would think him crazy. *Maybe I should keep these thoughts and dreams to myself,* he wondered silently.

The medicine woman handed him a large bowl filled with a cornmeal stew, which he began to devour hungrily. Having listened to his story about his incredible journey, she began to wonder just what lay beyond the stars. She was told to worship the gods, and this young man in front of her had spoken directly to them. She had just as many questions as the elders but didn't want to overwhelm the poor man. He was still healing from his injuries.

"I didn't realize how hungry I was. Thank you so much," Qaletaqa said, breaking her out of her thoughts.

Aki raised her eyes. She was unsure if she should look at this warrior who impressed her father and the elders so profoundly. She even wondered if he were some heavenly Spirit, such was the reverence among her tribe for him.

Ridiculous, she thought. *This is a simple brave like the rest of the thoughtless young men here. Handsome, certainly. But a Spirit from another world? That seems unlikely.*

"Are you feeling better?" she asked.

Qaletaqa considered what "better" meant at this point as he swallowed another bite of warm stew. "I'm exhausted. I feel like I could sleep for a week. Yet I feel like I just woke."

"You must rest more after your meal," Aki replied. "It sounds like you have been on a great journey for a long time. You have injuries that need to heal, especially your head."

She had to look away as she made this last remark so he couldn't see her smile. "It will take time for your body to renew. Even a Spirit must rest sometimes," she mused.

A curious choice of words, he thought. Qaletaqa wanted to say that he was no different from her. But was he? So much had happened so quickly that he was still trying to figure it out.

He thanked her for the food, handed her the empty bowl, and lay back down.

His head was reeling with all that he had been through. But was it real or his imagination? He made up his mind to keep to himself while he recovered. *I probably already made a fool of myself.*

Qaletaqa closed his eyes and drifted off.

***

Beaver Island was buzzing over the warrior from the Spirit world who blessed them with his presence. Aki overheard all the others talk about Qaletaqa while she was gathering some supplies.

"He must be a god," said one warrior.

"He looks like a god," mused a young girl as she giggled. All those around her broke into laughter and hoots.

"My grandfather said he came to us from the Spirit world, so he must be some type of God. Maybe even the Kitche Manitou, the Great Spirit," said another young girl.

The same hushed whispers engrossed the entire tribe throughout the day.

Qaletaqa tried to force himself from his flat position several times that day. Still, his weary body and mind continued pushing his eyes closed again.

The gentle touch of the lovely woman who was attending to him, whose eyes were kind and inviting, helped lull him into a restful state that allowed him to fall asleep. When he started to move around and look like he was going to get up, she gently pressed his body into the warm fur of his bedding and whispered in his ear to calm down. He was enjoying the closeness with her. He wished those calming eyes would be there to welcome him to consciousness each time he opened his own eyes.

Her eyes are as dark as the midnight sky and filled with as much sparkle, Qaletaqa thought.

He enjoyed watching her willowy body move around the hut in a graceful dance. She effortlessly rose to a standing position after fussing over him, then deftly flowed about the small hut, gathering herbs and food to help with his healing.

She continued to protect him from the elders and other curious eyes of the tribe. He was pleased with that, as he enjoyed his time alone with her. They talked about their tribes and the differences between them. He was thrilled when Aki asked about his family and life before his adventure. He happily told her his story, at times shyly boasting of how brave a hunter he was. He told her his existence was different after everything he had learned from his Spirit teachers. He voiced his concerns about killing an animal now. He felt it would be difficult.

As Aki listened, her interest increased. Even though she spent her childhood listening to her parents and other elders talk about gods and the Spirit world, she never felt like she could truly understand it. Before she actually witnessed it with her own eyes she had the preconceived notion that it was just a story told to children in order to influence their behavior.

She recounted the events that led to her becoming known as the medicine woman. She explained that the skill of learning about various medicinal herbs from her mother, grandmother, and great-grandmother was something that had been passed down to her throughout her family. She revealed to him that she had never met her great-grandmother but that she frequently dreamed of her. In particular, when she required assistance in determining how to treat a condition with which she was not familiar and needed advice. Her great-grandmother would never fail to come through for her at the right moment when she needed assistance.

She had an innate understanding of the art of healing, which was almost like having magical powers. In some cases, she was unable to explain how or even why she had the ability to heal. She just did.

"It's your gift to this world," Qaletaqa told her. "This is why you are so good at it. The gods have given you this special gift."

"In my village, we had no one like you, but we heard about great healers. They are called Mide," Qaletaqa explained.

"You must be a Mide, Aki. You are said to have a special relationship with all Spirits. You certainly have a gift. Maybe you could teach others how to heal as well as you."

"I don't know about that, Qaletaqa. I'm nothing special. I've just learned a lot from my family, and it's what I enjoy doing more than anything else."

"Exactly," he said, excitement creeping into his voice. "It's what you enjoy more than anything else, and you're naturally good at it. It's your gift to the world. You and I are alike in that we should share gifts with others on Earth."

"Shhhh, Qaletaqa. Be calm and lie back down," Aki stopped him. "We can talk about this later. You must continue to rest."

Aki turned away from him, her face flushed with emotion. This brave God, or whoever he was, at least had kind words and encouragement that the braves in her tribe never cared to acknowledge.

He believes in me, she thought. *Just my luck. An intelligent man who washes up on the beach takes an interest in my work and believes in me. This must be a dream.*

Aki agreed with the women in the tribe who said he was a good-looking young man. He was very handsome. She would be blind not to notice that. But she liked him even more as he seemed genuinely interested in her and her life here.

It was strange that his tribe didn't have a medicine man or woman. She always assumed there was someone in each village who could help treat wounds and would make concoctions to heal ailments.

He was probably interested in what she did because he had never had someone take care of him like this before. She wasn't doing anything special, just what she knew she needed to do. And yet he called her knowledge a gift, which caused a little bubble of excitement to grow in her stomach.

There were people in this tribe that took her for granted. She was just a plain woman who healed. But to Qaletaqa, she saved lives and made a difference. He gave her confidence in herself about what she was capable of.

***

Toward evening, Qaletaqa finally felt strong enough to crawl from under the warm furs and stand upright. Aki quickly objected, but Qaletaqa was too curious to see more of this new tribe.

He was unsteady on his feet initially, then tentatively moved toward the hut's opening. Aki steadied him as she leaned in under his arm. He opened the flap of the hut and stepped out to find he was immediately the center of attention.

Qaletaqa was met with wondrous stares from the tribe members who saw him as they walked through the camp attending to chores.

They looked up from stoking fires, carrying vegetables, and hauling hides and wood. He knew he looked different from them because he was from a distant tribe. There were physical differences, like the style of face paint and the color of his clothing. But the true distinction was in the way he conducted himself.

He knew he was a talented hunter and warrior. He carried that confidence in himself, and even though he was wounded, he still wanted to be that strong young man his tribe knew him for.

Still, despite his urgency to connect with them, he was surprised they wouldn't approach him. They seemed content to look at him with admiration.

"They think of you as a god," Aki whispered to Qaletaqa. "They are unsure of how to talk to you."

Qaletaqa simply nodded in understanding and gave a warm smile to everyone as they returned to their work.

Qaletaqa took a couple of shaky steps as his legs adjusted to walking again after several days on his back. Aki didn't leave his side. He was struck by how busy this tribe was. Everyone was running around preparing for a festival, which he assumed was typical for this tribe.

Young warriors were starting a fire in a pit at the center of the village. Other tribe members were hanging decorations in the trees surrounding their wigwams and on the wigwams themselves. The women painted children's faces in shades of red, yellow, and, most significantly, white—the color of peace.

An elder noticed Qaletaqa and quickly approached. Qaletaqa remembered him from the questioning a few days ago and was happy to speak to him again.

"How are you?" the elder asked.

"Better. I feel my strength returning," Qaletaqa said with a smile.

"If you're feeling well enough, we would be honored if you would join us at the celebration," the elder asked.

"I would be honored," Qaletaqa replied. He was excited to see how this tribe celebrated. This was indeed a wonderful gift for him. "What is the celebration for?"

"It is for you," the man replied. "We are honored that you came to share the Spirit world with us. We will celebrate into the night if you are our guest."

"For me?" Qaletaqa said modestly. "You should not celebrate me. I am no different from you."

But before he could object, the elder lightly took Qaletaqa's arm from Aki and guided him to the ceremonial seat near the fire. Aki kneeled at his side, ready to protect him from overly curious tribe members.

Numerous warriors dressed as elk, wolves, and brown bear danced around the fire as the evening wore on into the night, and the fire roared to a higher level of intensity. The pelts of a wide variety of animals hung loosely from their strong, agile bodies and swayed in time with the rhythm of their dance. The ground shook as members of the tribe swayed in response to the loud, pulsing rhythm produced by the drums.

Their appearance was obscured by masks, and some of them even had the heads of animals perched atop their brow. The dim light cast by the blazing fire gave the impression that the heads were alive. But everyone's focus was on their visitor, Qaletaqa, the God who had traveled all the way from the Spirit world to be with them.

***

Onadaga stayed in the shadows with his friends.

He could see that Aki never left the young man's side. The man would lean over and whisper something to her. Then she would place a hand on his leg and respond. They seemed too comfortable with each other. He felt jealousy rage from inside of him.

This was not how things were supposed to happen. It was he that she was supposed to be fawning over. She was supposed to be at his side, not this stranger who spoke of an epic journey to the Spirit world.

"Look at these fools celebrating a strange tribesman who washed up on our beach claiming to have traveled from the heavens. They have been smoking too much peace pipe, I'd say. Some God. He can barely walk. If he were a god, why does he have injuries like a common brave?"

His friends laughed and poked fun at him, commenting on how much time his favorite female spent in the medicine hut nursing this stranger back to health. They wondered aloud what else they might have done in there.

Onadaga seethed at his friends.

"You're all fools if you think he will be around here long enough to become friendly with my Aki. I'll send that so-called "god" back to where he came from with an arrow in his chest."

Chapter 10
Keep the Light

The weeks had flown by, and Qaletaqa had healed from his injuries. He had kept himself entertained with the villagers, who all wanted to know the secrets of the Spirit world. The elders were curious about what he had gone through, asking questions about the gods that he had met and the seven planes. The children wanted to hear about his life back in his village, his brothers, and his mother.

His words entranced everyone, and Qaletaqa secretly enjoyed all the attention he was receiving. He loved telling his stories and sharing what he had experienced on his journey. But there was that nagging part in his mind that said he needed to do more. He needed more people to hear about his experiences and what lay beyond life on Earth.

As tough as the decision was, he knew he had to move on and share his experience with many more.

He felt good about his health and condition; he had even ventured out on a hunt with some other warriors from the village. They were thrilled to have the "luck of the gods" with them, as they put it. They returned with more meat than they ever had before. Even years later, after Qaletaqa left, they still told stories about hunting with the God who called in the animals so quickly for them to take.

Qaletaqa spent extra time with Aki. Not because he was ill or needed more medical attention but because he enjoyed her presence. They talked for hours while hiking through the forest to find berries, roots, and herbs that Aki used to heal her tribe. He found her fascinating. She was brilliant and well-respected in her village. She gave so much to them and asked for so little in return. She was wonderful.

They spent hours talking about their families and the origins of their tribes. She explained her clan's legends of Nanabozo, a shapeshifter who was the embodiment of life, with the power to create life in others. Her grandmother had shared stories of Nanabozo making unique plants that emitted oils to cure sickness and disease. He created animals that were givers of their lives so that clans could survive the harsh winters of the great lake territory.

Aki shared those stories with such enthusiasm that Qaletaqa always asked for more. He wanted to learn everything he could from her and be around her.

Aki explained how every large geographic structure, be it a rock, boulder, tall tree, or large hill, constituted a possible malevolent Manitou that brought sickness, misfortune, or death. These landmarks had to be treated with respect, which is why she always carried tobacco as an offering to the Manitou.

Aki enjoyed Qaletaqa's company as well. Other tribe members talked about her hogging the special Spirit, Qaletaqa. Thinking they were crazy, she turned a deaf ear.

She didn't ask Qaletaqa to join or talk with her; he always seemed to be there. At first, she was annoyed because she did enjoy searching for herbs on her own. Still, she eventually found herself enjoying his companionship. It also made her less worried about predators or other dangers. Qaletaqa was a strong warrior who kept his guard up. Even though she felt at ease in the forest and with animals, there was still the fear of other people. It made Aki think of what happened with Onadaga.

Obviously, Onadaga didn't like Qaletaqa being around at all. He hated how much time this new brave spent with her. Aki could feel the anger radiate when she caught a glimpse of him. His arms were crossed over his chest, and his face was puffed out.

She was worried about him and what he might do. That was why she was glad to have Qaletaqa around her so much. Beyond talking, it kept Onadaga at bay.

One afternoon, after taking a short rest in his bed, Qaletaqa sought out Aki. He had some things on his mind, and he was hoping that she would help him out. Ever since he had gone to the Spirit world, he had wanted to write down the eleven truths he had learned. He found it difficult since he had so many ideas running through his mind, and he hoped that Aki would help him organize them in a teachable way.

It didn't take long for Qaletaqa to find Aki. She was generally around her hut, where she performed her healing, or on a trek to find more herbs. With the winter months arriving soon, she was gathering up as much as possible; the bushes and trees wouldn't be accessible through all the snow.

He let himself into the hut and saw her making a list of items she currently had. She would point to the items on the table and count in her head, then create symbols for her inventory. Qaletaqa knew right then and there that he had chosen the right person to help him out.

"Aki," he spoke hesitantly. Not startled by his presence, she looked up and smiled at him.

"Qaletaqa, how are you today?" Aki asked. While they usually spent the better part of their days together, Aki had a tribe member who needed her attention this morning. They were feeling congested in their nose and had watery eyes, which seemed to plague many tribe members during spring and summer months.

"I'm well," Qaletaqa replied. "I hoped I didn't bother you just now."

"Oh no," Aki laughed. "I'm always checking what I have and what I need. You aren't interrupting me." Qaletaqa sighed in relief.

"I wanted to speak to you and wondered if you could help me with something." Aki listened and nodded her head to allow Qaletaqa to continue.

"Ever since I returned from the Spirit world, so much has been going through my head. I have so many thoughts and lessons I learned, and I can't seem to put them in order," Qaletaqa explained. Aki nodded again, listening to what he was saying. Aki still had some reservations about what Qaletaqa had gone through, but she knew it was always best to get your thoughts out when you were working through something.

"I have come up with eleven truths that I believe all people should live by. I plan to visit all the villages and teach them these truths so that everyone can become better people and do well on this plane of existence," Qaletaqa explained. "I was hoping you could help me figure out the best way to explain these truths or just help me write them down so that I may teach them to others."

Their common language was symbols and images of things as they spoke differently. This was one of the ways they were able to communicate when Qaletaqa first came to the tribe. If there were words he didn't know, she would point to the object or draw him a picture. It helped bridge the gap between them.

"Of course, Qaletaqa," Aki replied. "I would like to help you with that."

Chapter 11
Eleven Truths

Qaletaqa and Aki sat down on the floor, discussing where to start. Qaletaqa talked a mile a minute, and his ideas were all over the place. Aki realized she needed to help guide him, just like she would with her patients. When someone was ill, they would talk about their pains or how they felt everywhere. She learned to listen but also to direct her questions to specific things so that she could better understand what was wrong.

"Qaletaqa, you need to slow down," Aki calmly said. Qaletaqa stopped speaking. "You said there were eleven truths. We need to do these one at a time." Qaletaqa nodded in agreement and was about to start speaking again, but Aki interrupted him.

"We need to start at the most important. If you were to teach someone only one of these truths, which would it be?" Aki asked. Qaletaqa seemed to ponder that for a moment.

There were a lot of truths he learned from the Spirit world. It was hard to pinpoint an exact one, but he suddenly came to the idea of light.

"We are light," Qaletaqa began. "We are nothing but light. Light is our energy. Light is our source. Light is our connection to the world beyond. Light is everything, and we see nothing but light when we concentrate internally."

Qaletaqa continued, "We can follow the light to worlds beyond through meditation. Worlds that we have come from before our experience on Earth. Worlds from which our life energy originates. We replenish our daily energy from this light source when we sleep."

"Where does this refreshed energy come from?" Aki asked. "All you were doing was sleeping. How does sleep give you energy?"

Qaletaqa smiled. "When you are so tired that you can't go on, you sleep. When you wake, you are refreshed and full of energy once again. This happens every day." Aki nodded in understanding.

"This energy is from the light, your source. The source replenishes your energy in dreamless sleep. So, when you sleep soundly, your light—or Spirit—goes back to the source, and the source replenishes your energy," Qaletaqa added.

"But we receive energy from food and water and sunlight?" Aki asked.

"Yes, but most of your energy is delivered directly from the source while you are in a dreamless sleep," Qaletaqa replied. "And it isn't just in sleep. You can connect directly with this light energy whenever you desire during quiet, deep meditation."

"I think that is perfect for being the first truth," Aki praised Qaletaqa. "What would you say is the second truth?"

Qaletaqa thought again for a moment and came up with the connection. "We are all connected. Every living thing is part of the same energy source."

Qaletaqa continued, "You are Spiritually connected to your family, friends, tribal members, neighboring tribes, and people across the world. You are Spiritually connected to your pets and other animals, every species, flower, plant, and tree."

"How can we be connected to those we have never met? Or animals that we must kill for food?" Aki questioned.

"We are all an intimate part of each other through our source energy, the light. We are here to love everything and everyone," Qaletaqa explained. Aki turned her head away.

"What if we can't love everyone? What if there are people too cruel for this world?" Aki asked.

"Then I would say the next truth should be about accepting ourselves. We are more than our ego," Qaletaqa stated. "You identify every day with the person you see. Yet the face and body you recognize every day are not you. It's simply your ego or how you perceive yourself. You want to rise above that."

"Consider yourself as only light energy currently having a human experience. This is accomplished by living in the present. Forget about what happened to you yesterday, which shaped your ego. Forget about and stop worrying about the future, which you cannot change. Live today, only today, only this minute. Because that's all there really is," Qaletaqa said. He looked at Aki, who was busy writing down what she could.

Her last question seemed odd, but perhaps it was a more general question than something else. She had never left her tribe before, so maybe there was someone here that was not good. Perhaps something had happened…the fourth truth came to mind.

"The fourth truth should be: accept what happened, then strive to change," Qaletaqa blurted out. Aki looked up at him because they had been quiet for a moment until he suddenly blurted that out. She nodded at him to continue his explanation.

"Live in complete acceptance of what has happened to you or your loved ones, but always strive to change and improve. What has happened to you cannot change because it was supposed to happen in your life for one reason or another.

You can't change it, so let it go and move on with your life," Qaletaqa spoke.

"We're just supposed to accept things that happen. That seems odd," Aki replied.

"We will never understand why things happen the way they do. Why did a loved one get sick or die? Why did we lose everything in a storm? Why did we fall in love with certain people? Why do we have to deal with a debilitating disease? Why is my child ill? You, Aki, probably see this a lot, and you may never understand," Qaletaqa explained. "Maybe years from now, it may become clear why something happened to you or someone else. It's part of a master plan we may not understand during our lifetime on Earth. You can't change what happened and may never know why until you are back in the Spirit world."

"Whatever happens, be it hardship or blessing, you must accept it and move on. Don't let it control the rest of your life." Qaletaqa looked straight at Aki as he spoke the last part. She looked at him from her paper and saw he was directing his statement toward her. He didn't realize just how much she needed to hear those words.

Just then, a warrior came in with some cuts along his arms. He and a few others had been through the dense woods, tracking a deer, and the branches had left their mark on him. Aki welcomed the man and looked toward Qaletaqa.

"We can work on this some more in a little while. I'll need some time with these wounds," she explained. Qaletaqa nodded to both Aki and the man. He knew that Aki took her work seriously, which he admired greatly about her. He took his leave and walked around a bit, gathering his thoughts about the following few truths.

***

Aki couldn't find Qaletaqa again until after dinner. She had spent some time with the injured brave and ensured that nothing would get infected. She and Qaletaqa sat together, but they only talked about what she did for the warrior and what herbs she used.

Some other tribe members came to speak with Qaletaqa and ask him questions about the Spirit world. Qaletaqa was more than happy to talk about that and even used some of the truths he and Aki had worked on together.

Aki could see the passion in his eyes as he spoke about being connected to one another and that we were all made of light. It was refreshing to see someone so focused on something and enjoy it. She was used to seeing her fellow tribe members become what they were expected to be. The men grew to be strong warriors and hunters. The women tended to the food and children. It was a mediocre life, and everyone had just learned to accept it for what it was.

Aki was fortunate enough to have a family who was experienced in medicine. It gave her a sense of purpose in this life and allowed her to be the person she wanted to be.

Once dinner was over and everyone went back to their huts, Qaletaqa followed Aki back to hers, where they could continue their work.

"I believe the fifth truth should be to live with peace. It's much easier to be peaceful than stressed. So, choose to be peaceful," Qaletaqa spoke. Aki smiled.

"That sounds very easy to you," Aki joked.

"It sounds simple because it is," Qaletaqa teased her back. "If we were all to choose peace in every situation we encounter, we would all get along better and live happier lives. When people become stressed with new situations, they change to their regular behavior patterns. If they were to accept the changes with peace instead of refusal or rebuttal, wouldn't that be better?" Qaletaqa questioned. "Most of the time, we can't change the situation anyway."

"I agree. We must not fight fate, as it will happen anyway. We need to embrace the change," Aki replied.

"Exactly!" Qaletaqa exclaimed. "We need to live life with grace, peace, and lightness." Aki continued to write as Qaletaqa spoke.

"The sixth truth is that everything that arises passes away," Qaletaqa stated. "Every life passes on sooner or later, before or after you. You will pass, your family and children will pass, your friends and acquaintances will pass, your pets will pass, and your plants and flowers will also pass on to the light source."

"I have seen that happen," Aki responded.

"And It's just a part of life," Qaletaqa spoke. "We need to embrace that life begins and ends. By not accepting that, we are choosing the opposite. A life of hardship, drudgery, and drama."

"I once had a day when an older woman died in the tribe with no illness. She simply did not wake. And later, a woman had a baby. Some saw this new life and grew excited. While others saw the loss of life and became sad," Aki explained. "I felt both. But I knew with the end of one life, there was a new life just beginning.

"That is how we should live our lives. Death is sad, and we should grieve, but we should also know that it was bound to happen at one point. We cannot stop what the Spirits have in store for us. We should cherish and love the people we are with while we are still here," Qaletaqa replied.

"I think that truly spoke to me deeper than the others. I live my days waiting for death and the new life of my tribe. It's hard to accept, but I accept it more easily now," Aki said.

"I believe that goes with the seventh truth, that we must flow with life," Qaletaqa spoke. "How many times have you had a hunch that you should be doing something or going a different direction, but you decided not to follow that hunch only to realize that it would have made a difference in your life?"

"A few times," Aki smiled.

"We should learn to follow hunches. Flow with the inner thoughts that you know are right for you, going with life's current rather than fighting it," Qaletaqa continued. "These are our Spirit guides, and we should listen to them. They are leading you on the right path. They are the voice in your head, helping you to make the best decisions. Not only is it the right path, but it's also the peaceful path in your life."

"So those times when I think I should be going another direction or when I feel like danger is ahead?" Aki asked.

"Those are the Spirits looking after you," Qaletaqa explained. "Run your life on Spiritual energy, not recommendations from those who don't understand you and your life path. Your Spirit guides know exactly who you are and want the best for you."

"I dream of my grandmother; she tells me things I need to know. The right herbs or the right medicines to use," Aki admitted. "Is she guiding me?"

"Absolutely. Probably more than just medicine. She might be telling you which friends to have or people to connect with," Qaletaqa said. Aki nodded in understanding. She then let out a yawn and covered her mouth in embarrassment.

"I guess it's getting late. We should stop for now and do more tomorrow," Aki said.

"I agree. Thank you again for helping me with this," Qaletaqa replied. "Have a good night."

"Good night, Qaletaqa." Aki waited until Qaletaqa had almost reached his own hut before closing the door on hers. She was exhausted, but her mind still felt very much awake. She looked over the papers that she had drawn on and remembered the first truth of being light and re-energizing ourselves with sleep. Perhaps she would try meditation to clear her mind and allow her body to recharge.

***

When Qaletaqa stepped into her hut the next morning, Aki was happy to see him. She had been awake and busy for quite some time, and she had him to thank for that.

"I tried meditating yesterday, and it worked so well," Aki exclaimed before Qaletaqa could say a word. "I cleared my mind and just concentrated on the sounds around me, and I fell asleep so quick."

"You must have a gift for meditation. It usually takes others a long time to learn how to clear their mind," Qaletaqa replied. Aki smiled at him. They took their spots on the floor again as Qaletaqa began to speak about the next truth.

"The next one needs to be about love," Qaletaqa began. "We should feel love in our hearts every day. We all want love, we crave love, and we all know the feeling of love, whether it be love for a significant other in your life, love for a child or parent, or love for a pet."

Qaletaqa continued, "It's the best feeling in the world, in this world and beyond. We need to practice sending love everywhere, even to those unfortunate beings who only have anger to send out into the world. Send them love. It will make a profound difference in their life and yours."

"You woke up in a good mood today, too," Aki pointed out. Qaletaqa blushed slightly.

"I think I feel lighter," he admitted. "Getting these thoughts out and talking through them with you has helped clear my mind. I know what I want to say and how to say it and how to teach this to others."

"It's very noble of you to want to teach others."

"I am only doing what was asked of me. I want to follow through on this journey and wherever it takes me," Qaletaqa admitted.

"Well, what is the ninth truth then?" Aki asked.

It took Qaletaqa a moment, but he replied. "Life is an illusion. It is only the first plane of existence."

"So, is this life experience real? Do we remember this part?" Aki inquired.

"It feels real, down to the second," Qaletaqa replied.

"But if we are simply light energy having a human experience, then who are we?" Aki asked again.

"That is the question we should concentrate on every day. Who are we, really? What are we? The light energy that keeps us alive is doing so for what reason? Why do we have a human experience?" Qaletaqa questioned back. "There is an obvious reason, which some of us may not figure out until our light energy moves on to the next dimension."

"What is the reason?" Aki asked impatiently.

"Many have figured it out through deep, inquisitive thought and meditation. These are the people among us who live life easier in the knowledge that they are accomplishing on Earth what they were sent here for," Qaletaqa explained. "Consequently, they know that life is an illusion. They know that they are only here temporarily to help mankind in a way that is unique to them and that only they have the gift to do just what they were sent here for."

"Death is also an illusion to them, so they have no need to worry about life and death. Your energy force of life continues forever," Qaletaqa stated.

"So, we need to remember that we go on beyond this," Aki stated rather than questioned.

"Absolutely, there is so much beyond our world, and this life that we are living right now is just a small part of that."

"So, we need to accept this life for what it is and live peacefully amongst everyone else?" Aki questioned.

"And happiness. That is the tenth truth. To choose happiness," Qaletaqa replied.

"That again sounds so easy to say," Aki stated.

"It sounds simple, and it is if you train your mind," Qaletaqa agreed. "We encounter a wide range of emotions, from happiness to anger to sadness to elation and everything in between, sometimes in a short span of time."

"It is your choice to live your life in the emotion you choose. You can choose to be angry all the time and live a life of anger, upsetting everyone you encounter and making yourself and others miserable. But why? Why would anyone choose to live a life of anger? It's often because we don't understand. Such people don't understand that the choice is theirs," Qaletaqa continued.

"Life on Earth is too short to live in anger when happiness is also a choice. When you are happy, you make others happy, including yourself. The happier you choose to be, the happier you become, and it becomes a habit. It is easier said than done, but like any other habit, it becomes a practice."

"So those who are angry and mean just choose to be like that?" Aki asked.

"There are plenty of excuses to not see happiness as a possibility because of daily changes and life experiences, like illness, depression, tragic accidents, and even the death of friends and loved ones. One needs to see past that and accept those things and choose happiness," Qaletaqa clarified.

"Alright, I think that makes sense. What would be the last truth then?" Aki inquired.

"Meditate, of course," Qaletaqa laughed. "There is nothing more important in this life experience than quiet reflection into your soul. Quieting your mind allows you to live the truths of the Spirit world. This is also the key to realizing why you have a human experience."

"I thought you should clear your mind when meditating," Aki asked.

"You should focus while meditating. Whether you be quiet or focused on a specific question. Like, what is your mission to accomplish on Earth? What special gift do you have that can help all of mankind?" Qaletaqa continued. "A form of quiet reflection, be it prayer or meditation, will allow you to find your Spirit gift. There are many forms of self-reflection. Choose one that is comfortable for you and use it every day. The world is waiting for you to share your Spirit gift and help mankind."

"A Spirit gift?" Aki looked confused.

"That is for you to find out. I think you already know the gift that has been given to you. You should share it with the world. That is what everyone should do."

"It may not be possible to do that, though," Aki stated.

"You can make anything possible. You must have the right mindset to do it," Qaletaqa explained.

"Well, I think we got them all now," Aki said, changing the subject quickly. She knew what Qaletaqa was trying to do and say, and she just wasn't ready to think about that yet.

"Can I see what we've come up with?" Qaletaqa asked. Aki handed the paper to Qaletaqa so he could look over the eleven truths.

1. **We Are Light**
2. **We Are All Connected**
3. **We Are More Than Our Ego**
4. **Accept What Happened, Then Strive to Change**
5. **Live With Peace**
6. **Everything That Arises Passes Away**
7. **Flow With Life**
8. **Love**
9. **Life Is An Illusion**
10. **Choose Happiness**
11. **Meditate**

"This is it, Aki. This is what I want to teach," Qaletaqa said proudly. He smiled at Aki, who returned the gesture. "Thank you so much for helping me with this. I truly appreciate it."

"It has been my pleasure, Qaletaqa," Aki replied. "This helped me to understand your journey a little better."

"Now, I can't wait to share this with everyone." Qaletaqa's smile grew in excitement. He felt like this was the starting point of his new journey. He would spread the truths of this life and tell the world how wonderful their lives could be.

Chapter 12

Let Love Fill Your Heart

Winter arrived in a burst of Arctic cold and snow flurries on Bered Island. The deepening snow cover always made foraging for food more difficult. To reproduce in these polar climes, snow family called them Pari. Most animals hibernated as a result, and others stayed within the helpful solar thermal heat reach of people and trees searchers looking for food. The winters were just too long for hibernation to become totally a harsh winter.

Members of the folks were trapped in the fallen trees and uprooted wetlands with them, hindered by the ice that blanketed the horizon, rapid ice movement. Even the hunt was supposed. The arduous task of carrying the cargo and loading — not of them dangerous areas was not worth it.

Odeaga helped out now, that he was strong as till. The men are wanted him on every hunt to guide them, but

137

Chapter 12

Let Love Fill Your Heart

Winter arrived in a burst of familiar cold, and snow blanketed Beaver Island. The deepening snow, as always, made foraging for food more difficult. It was common in these parts to have snow drifts taller than any man. Most animals hibernated as a result, and others stayed within the sheltered cedar swamps, out of reach of people and other predators looking for food. The wetlands were just too tricky for tribe members to navigate during a harsh winter.

Members of the tribe were kept out by fallen trees and ice-covered wetlands with rivers covered by thin ice that unsuspecting hunters could fall through. Even if a hunt was successful, the arduous task of retrieving the game and hauling it out of these dangerous areas was not worth it.

Qaletaqa helped out now that he was strong again. Tribe members wanted him on every hunt to guide them, and

Qaletaqa obliged as much as he could though he didn't like being away from Aki.

There had been a moment on one of their walks that troubled him. What worried him was Onadaga and his jealousy of Aki. He felt this pull and connection to Aki and believed she felt something too.

He always seemed to be watching from far away but still within sight distance. No matter where he and Aki went, Onadaga was always nearby. If they left the village to hunt for herbs, he would stand by the perimeter and await their return. If they were talking around the fire as everyone ate their meal, he could feel Onadaga's eyes on him.

Qaletaqa was unsure how to bring this up with Aki. Maybe he hadn't heard of their engagement, or maybe Aki had been promised to him long ago. Qaletaqa would surely put aside his own feelings if it meant that he didn't interfere with their relationship. Although, from the way Aki was around Onadaga, it didn't seem like she favored a relationship with him.

If Aki caught Onadaga watching them, she would immediately move away from him. If he tried to sit near them for meals, Aki would turn the other way. He didn't understand her unwillingness to be around him and continued to stalk her like a hunter to its prey. It was almost like she was trying to hide from him.

She doesn't seem comfortable around him, Qaletaqa thought. *I wonder if something happened to her.*

She tried to hide her feelings about Onadaga with more stories. Still, Qaletaqa could see that something was bothering her. Qaletaqa decided he would ask her about it.

***

It was a cold, brisk morning as Qaletaqa left his hut. He managed to find a bed with another young warrior from the tribe. His brother had gone on his own quest and wouldn't be back until the spring. Qaletaqa was glad to not live in the medicine hut anymore, but it also meant seeing Aki a little less.

The tribe had been so giving to Qaletaqa and gave him the proper clothing to wear in the winter. Animal pelts and leather shoes protected him from the harsh winds and cold ground. He didn't believe he earned their generosity, but they were adamant that he did. He brought good fortune to them for hunting and gathering, and the stories of his journey to the Spirit world filled them with the knowledge they would have never known.

Because the snow covered the ground, Qaletaqa knew Aki would be working on her healing elixirs in the medicine hut. She had wood and tree branches on the floor, waiting to have their bark pulled off so she could use them for bandages.

She would grind the herbs into a paste and place them into pots.

Qaletaqa had learned a lot from Aki about treating illnesses and injuries. He encouraged her to share her gift with others, just like he was planning to in the spring. Although she seemed hesitant as she was needed here, he kept telling her how wonderful it would be for her to do it.

Aki sat on the hut's floor with animal pelts laid over to keep her warm. A light fire was burning in the corner, making the room feel warm. She turned her head to see Qaletaqa come in and gave him a welcoming smile.

"You slept in today," Aki joked with him. He was getting better at their language and could understand most of her words. Qaletaqa smiled.

"I had a lot to think about last night," Qaletaqa replied. "I've got to start planning so I'm ready when the spring comes." Qaletaqa could see Aki turn away. Perhaps it saddened her to know he would be leaving eventually.

"My tribe will provide you with whatever you need. You have done so much for us already," Aki spoke quietly. She continued to work and allowed Qaletaqa to stay with her.

After standing near the hut's entrance for a few moments, Qaletaqa finally sat down. He didn't look at her; he just touched some dried herbs on the floor.

"I wanted to ask you about Onadaga," Qaletaqa began and looked up to watch Aki's reaction. He saw her pause for the briefest moments, but she quickly returned to work. "I can tell he doesn't like me, and that anger seems to come from me being around you. Was there something between you two? An engagement or something?" Qaletaqa asked.

Aki laughed lightly. "He thought we should be married, yes. But I didn't want to," Aki responded.

"Did something happen between you two then?" he asked. Aki paused and looked at Qaletaqa.

"What do you mean?" Aki spoke with a severe tone, clearly not amused by this conversation. Qaletaqa thought maybe he shouldn't have said anything at all. But he thought back to what he had learned from the Spirits and knew he just needed to trust himself.

"I see how he looks at you and how you look at him. He looks possessive over you. And you look sick when you catch his eye," Qaletaqa explained. "I just want to better understand the relationship between you two."

Aki was angered by Qaletaqa's questions. She didn't want to tell him anything. Qaletaqa could tell that his words were not welcome. He was worried that she would throw him out and ask him to leave her alone.

"I'm sorry if I upset you. I just didn't want to cause trouble in your tribe," Qaletaqa explained. "I can tell you don't want to talk about it, but maybe I could tell you something instead." Qaletaqa waited for Aki to respond to him. When she didn't, he took that as a sign that she was willing to hear him talk.

"I met with my father's Spirit during my journey. He guided me through the fifth plane," Qaletaqa began. "The fifth plane is about filling your heart with love. He told me that love is more important than anything because with love filling your heart, there is no room for anything else." Qaletaqa paused to let that sink in. "I thought it meant loving all those around you and showing care and compassion. I realize now that it also means not letting anger and fear in your heart."

Qaletaqa continued, "Whatever happened, you shouldn't let the anger fill your heart. It overpowers the love that you carry inside and brings negativity to your life. You can live a wonderful life by being truthful and having a heart filled with love."

Aki bit her lip softly as she listened to Qaletaqa's words. She knew she had let a lot of anger toward Onadaga into her heart and mind. It had changed her, and now that Qaletaqa pointed it out, it hit her hard. A small tear fell from her eye.

"Onadaga has always thought of me as his bride. I told my father I would never marry someone like him, and he seemed to understand. Onadaga never understood," Aki spoke softly. Qaletaqa watched her and listened.

"Before you came here, I had been in the woods gathering supplies when I heard Onadaga sneak up behind me.

He told me we would be married and that our fathers had agreed. I was so mad and told him that I would never marry him." Aki paused as she took a slow breath. "He didn't like how I spoke and attacked me."

Qaletaqa froze at that moment. He shut his eyes and pushed away the anger he was now feeling. This wasn't about Onadaga; it was about Aki, and she needed a friend.

"Did he hurt you?" Onadaga asked. Aki nodded her head.

"He pulled at my clothes and tried to touch me," her voice wavered from the emotion as she thought back to that day. "There was a rock within my reach, and I hit him. He fell over and closed his eyes. I ran away as fast as I could."

Qaletaqa now understood why she looked physically sick when she looked at Onadaga. She had done right, fighting back and getting away from him. He had done something so terrible; it was hard to even imagine.

"Did you tell anyone when you got back?" Qaletaqa questioned. Aki shook her head.

"No. I was so ashamed of what I had done. I thought that maybe I had killed him or left him hurt." Aki let a few more tears escape from the corners of her eyes. Qaletaqa knew that she had kept this bottled up for so long.

"You've held this secret for too long, Aki. You need to let it out," Qaletaqa responded. Aki spent the next few minutes crying and telling Qaletaqa how she felt. Onadaga told her he loved her, and yet he treated her so viscously. She felt violated and angry that he did that to her.

Qaletaqa just listened and let her get all the anger and hostility out. She was speaking her truth, and Qaletaqa knew just how important that was. When she finally finished, and the tears were wiped away, she looked at Qaletaqa and gave him a smile.

"Thank you," she said.

"Why are you thanking me?" Qaletaqa asked. He was baffled as to why she felt like she needed to thank him.

"For reminding me to be truthful to myself and allowing others to help me when I need it," Aki stated. Qaletaqa reached out his hand toward her so she could grab it. When she touched his hand, he grasped it softly in comfort.

In his heart, Qaletaqa knew that this moment had turned their friendship into something else. He wasn't sure what it was yet, but he wanted to find out.

***

As dark winter months gave way to spring, Qaletaqa could enjoy long walks with Aki. They resumed their pursuit of plants and herbs that sprouted up in the warming days. The northern woods came alive with white trillium flowers, wild mushrooms, leeks, and bright-green foliage everywhere. The winter snow nourished the abundant spring growth, and Aki needed help with her harvest. Warm summer days with plentiful food were close at hand.

Qaletaqa could feel in his heart that the time had come for him to leave. He didn't know what lay before him. He knew he needed to return to the mainland and make his way back to his own tribe and to the family he missed. He wasn't entirely sure what he was to do, but a tug at his soul told him he must continue on his journey.

***

Saying goodbye to Aki was difficult. There was something so familiar about her, so comforting. True, he had spent much time getting to know her. But the ease with which they communicated hinted to him that something was deeper. He felt as if he had known Aki somewhere before.

So strange, he thought. *I just met her. I've never been here before, and she has never been off this island.*

Qaletaqa brushed away these thoughts and continued his goodbyes around the camp.

With Aki, it was more personal. She had been his caretaker in the early days of his arrival. She took care of him while he was vulnerable and alone. She befriended him.

Qaletaqa took her warm, soft hands and looked her in the eye as he said goodbye. Energy pulsed through his veins, and his heart pumped quickly.

He told her he hoped they would meet again, even though he was unsure. His hands had trouble letting go. His body kept telling him something. A voice in his head was saying something, but he couldn't make it out. As he walked away, the pain in his heart grew, and he knew it would be some time before it subsided.

Aki felt the energy too. She had never felt anything like it before. Indeed, she was a little saddened to see Qaletaqa leave. After all, they had become good friends throughout his recovery. But he was simply a patient that she cared for.

That's all it is, she mused. *Nothing more. Don't be silly to think there is anything else.*

But this was completely different. A longing in her mind told her she did not want him to leave. *I'll never forget you,* Aki thought to herself as he slowly let go of her hand.

She quickly brushed away the feeling, said goodbye to Qaletaqa, and stepped aside.

Qaletaqa stood by the freshly made birch bark canoe that Chief Decomsie had granted to him, with the tribe coming to the shore to see him off.

Several elders came to the front of the crowd.

The oldest elder cleared his throat and shyly asked, "Great Qaletaqa, can you share with us a way in which we can continue to have the good fortune that you have brought us from the Spirits above?"

The elders stood still with patient respect.

Somewhat embarrassed, Qaletaqa took his time and thought through what to impart to these friends who saved his life and those that believed him to be remarkable. He could only think of sharing what was shared with him.

"I am no different from you, my friends. I simply expect to find abundance, and I do," Qaletaqa replied. "You can do the same. However, I would like to share what I vividly remember from my travels. Quite simply, the light! Just think of light. It is everything."

Qaletaqa continued, "You see the light from your fire. You see the light from the full moon overhead at night. You see the light from the sun that warms us throughout the day. There is another light. This light is from beyond the stars. This light is brighter and more vibrant than any light you have ever seen. This light is you. We are all made of this light, and this light gives us life and power beyond any power you have seen. More power than the strongest bear. More power than the fiercest storm to crash on these shores. This light gives you the power to accomplish anything you can dream of. And it is already within you and you and you."

He slowly pointed to every elder standing before him.

"You can find this light and tap into its power by simply sitting quietly, closing your eyes, and concentrating on the light you see in your mind. Make the light bigger and bigger and bigger until it encompasses your body and projects out to the stars. The light will always direct you down the path that life created for you. Only by using the light can you stay on your chosen path and change the world."

The gathered group was silent.

Qaletaqa was not sure how this message would be received. He spoke the words, but they seemed to emanate from something far more profound than his ordinary self.

The Chief finally spoke. "Young Qaletaqa, you are wise well beyond your years. You speak directly from the Spirit world. We are grateful that you chose to land on our shore and spend time with our people. We will follow your direction. Be safe on your journey."

Qaletaqa wordlessly nodded to him—he'd already said what he needed to say. He then pushed the canoe, generously loaded with provisions for the next leg of his journey, from the sandy shore and into knee-deep water. He climbed into the seat made of saplings and elk hide, took a stroke with his paddle, and turned with a hand held over his head in tribute to the elders. They responded with the same gesture. Qaletaqa was on his way.

Chapter 13
Breath of Life

Qaletaqa began his trek along the island's shoreline shaped like a beaver. He paddled quickly, following the coastline of that island, then cut across open water to the next in a pattern, gradually working his way east.

As the sun dipped at the end of the first day, Qaletaqa approached the last island in this chain of islands. As he paddled to shore, two tribal warriors appeared from the woods. He did not know what to expect from these warriors, so he kept his guard up. Although Aki's tribe had been welcoming, there was no way to know if other tribes would accept him as they did.

The warriors stood along the barrier of their island as Qaletaqa dragged his canoe up the stony shore. They held their spears in their hands, waiting to hear from this newcomer. He approached the warriors and said, "I travel from the island shaped like a great beaver. I mean you no harm." He held his hands up in peace. "My name is Qaletaqa and…"

Upon hearing the new arrival's name, both warriors stared in shock, quickly glanced at each other, and then dropped to their hands and knees in a worship position.

Qaletaqa was stunned. He was going to explain himself, but these men had already heard of him. He quickly reached down to the tribesmen and gently raised their heads so he could see their eyes. "Please rise. Don't be afraid. Why are you acting this way?"

"You are the great warrior from the Spirit world?" the taller brave asked.

"Yes, but I am no different than either of you. I may have traveled to the Spirit world, but that doesn't make me someone to be worshipped. I was granted knowledge to share," Qaletaqa explained. He turned toward the dimming sun and looked back at the men beginning to stand up again. "May I shelter in your village for a few nights?"

"Yes, of course," said the taller warrior. "I will escort you with your belongings. My brother will run ahead to get the village ready."

Qaletaqa nodded in humble appreciation as the brave left to prepare his village for the arrival of the great Spirit from another world.

The remaining warrior gathered Qaletaqa's supplies, heaping his arms and back with the skins and food. Qaletaqa asked that he be allowed to haul his own gear, but the warrior would not hear of it. He started off down a clear-cut path through the woods with Qaletaqa trailing.

He had just left Aki's tribe and had come across them within a day. Although they weren't far from each other, it felt quite new to him. Qaletaqa wondered how they were able to learn about him so quickly.

"May I ask how you knew who I was?" Qaletaqa asked the warrior beside him. The man looked back at Qaletaqa.

"We do trade with many tribes. Their gatherers talked about you and the things you learned from the Spirit world." Qaletaqa nodded in understanding. It would make sense that two tribes would offer trades of items with neighbors. Qaletaqa's tribe didn't have anyone nearby, so it was just them. Here, it seemed that plenty of islands could host friends and helping hands.

After a half-mile walk, they came to the village, the trail opening onto the compound. As Qaletaqa stepped into view, the tribe stared with curiosity. The Chief greeted him, standing with outstretched arms.

"We are very pleased you chose our village. Welcome, Qaletaqa," he said proudly. Qaletaqa felt that this tribe was proud to have someone like him come to visit. They all seemed interested to see him and talk with him. He guessed the encounter he had with Aki's tribe had really spread.

The tribe fawned over Qaletaqa, who was humbled and a little embarrassed. They prepared a feast for him, then escorted him to a teepee next to the Chief's. It was a luxurious accommodation in their eyes.

Around the fire, they asked him questions about his journey to the Spirit world and what lessons he had learned from the Spirits. Qaletaqa shared with the elders and the Chief the same message he had imparted to the last village. They were grateful to listen and take in his teachings.

The following day, the horizon was awash with red, orange, and yellow light cascading out of puffy, cumulus clouds. Qaletaqa and the tribe knew this was a bad sign. Such color often precedes windy, stormy conditions. He was unsure how long he would stay with this tribe, so he decided to stay another day, to the tribe's delight.

Another feast was prepared, and by noon the tribe sat around Qaletaqa as they enjoyed their meal indoors, hoping to learn more about his Spiritual journey and the world beyond.

"What message can you share with us from the Spirit world that can help all of us prosper?" the Chief asked.

Qaletaqa knew what he wanted to share but was apprehensive about how it would be received. It was something so simple that they may even laugh at him.

He quietly considered how to deliver this simple truth he had learned. He finally decided to tell it as it was and hoped his message was understood.

"You just need to breathe," Qaletaqa said succinctly.

There was no reaction from the gathered. He continued.

"I know it sounds unusual, but breath is life. And just as important, breath is energy. You must breathe deeply every minute of the day to fill your body with energy given to us by the great Spirits. You don't have to do anything special to obtain it. Just breathe. Do you notice that when you run a great distance, breathing heavily, you spend a lot of energy, yet you feel so alive afterward? The extra air you fill your body with gives you the energy to run but also fills you with more energy that makes you feel good after the run. Any time you breathe deeply, you can feel this extra heightened energy.

"The air we inhale with every breath is loaded with energy. Unfortunately, we are used to only breathing in shallow breaths during our daily activities. These shallow breaths only supply us with the minimum energy we need to survive. If you want more energy, concentrate on breathing deeply with every breath you take."

The tribesmen stared at Qaletaqa inquisitively. He could see in their eyes that they either didn't understand or thought he was joking.

"Let's look at it a different way," Qaletaqa said. "Do you notice that after a long day turns dark and you are exhausted, you start to yawn? Your body is telling you it is time to replenish your energy. So, you sleep. But when you wake to the morning sun, you are entirely refreshed with the energy to work and play hard all day again.

"Where did this new energy come from? The only thing you were doing was sleeping. However, you breathe very deep with long, slow breaths when you sleep. Some so deep and long that you sound like a bear."

The simplicity and starkness of the message elicited chuckles among the gathered. The bear reference had resonated.

One warrior said, "That sounds like my wife."

Qaletaqa smiled and waited for the laughter to subside. There was nothing wrong with adding humor to this message. He would do whatever it took to get them to understand.

"These deep breaths all night long are what supply you with energy for the next day," he continued. "Every night, you refresh your energy store just by deep breathing. It only makes sense that you can do the same to gain extra energy all day long."

An elder questioned Qaletaqa. "We have always believed that the food we eat from the corn we grow and the animals we hunt gives us the energy we need. Is this not true?"

"Yes," said Qaletaqa. "You receive needed energy from food and water, the vital energy we all need. However, are there days late in the snow months when there is little to eat?"

Heads nodded in agreement. One warrior said, "Of course, we feel hunger from lack of food."

"Right. But you still become tired at night, sleep, and you have refreshed energy to hunt at the next sunrise."

More nods of agreement.

"The air you breathed all night gave you that energy. You can't see the energy like you can see the food you eat and the water you drink, but it's there. I was taught in the Spirit world that the air we breathe contains tiny, unseen particles packed with energy. It is the Great Spirit's gift to us. Amazingly, almost all our energy comes from our breath. We supplement that with water, the same energy source, and food. Of course, we need all of these to survive. We forget how important breathing is, so you must concentrate on breathing as deep during the day as you automatically do while you sleep," Qaletaqa continued.

"But with all the activities we are involved in all day long, how do we stop to breathe?" a younger man asked.

"I have learned to begin my day sitting quietly and concentrating on deep breaths," Qaletaqa said. "This prepares me for the day and gives me even more energy. Now, I start my day with energy from my sleep and energy from deep breathing. This exercise also helps me remember to continue taking deep breaths throughout the day. It's not easy. Even though it's just breathing, it takes practice."

He added, "You must train yourself to take deep breaths often throughout the day, whether sitting quietly, eating a meal with others, conversing, or even in the middle of a hunt. Take a second to breathe deeply. Then take another and another. You will be amazed at how good this feels and how much added energy will course through your body at that moment.

"Soon, you will want to stop and breathe deeply and continuously. At this point, you will be living your life full of extra vibrant energy every day and enjoying the feeling of enjoying a full life."

The Chief was stern-faced as he was taking all this information in. Qaletaqa guessed that he was just someone who needed to take everything in. He tried to read the Chief's thoughts, but it was hard. The rest of the tribe nodded in understanding and talked to the people next to them about what Qaletaqa was saying.

Finally, the Chief gave a smile and nodded his head at Qaletaqa.

"Thank you, Qaletaqa," said the Chief as the session appeared to be closing. "Your wisdom from the Spirit world is a wonderful gift. We thank you for sharing this wisdom with us."

***

That evening gave way to a radiant sky of red and purple beams under wispy cirrus clouds. Red sky at night meant calm weather on the way, so Qaletaqa readied himself to continue his voyage that night.

He said his goodbyes and pushed off at sunset into the clear night. He knew the sky and could find the guiding bright North Star easily. He kept the star off his left shoulder as he paddled east across the expansive waters of Lake Michigan. The great lake was as smooth as a small inland pond with all its power and majesty. The night was calm.

Hour after laboring hour, Qaletaqa paddled.

As night gave way to morning, he looked up through the clear skies and was relieved to see the faint outline of land. Even though he was still miles away and would have to paddle for the better part of the day to get there, the mere sight of a tree line on the horizon gave him the motivation to paddle even more vigorously.

As Qaletaqa made his way back to the mainland from the islands, he took some time to think about what he had discussed with the members of the tribe who had come from the previous two villages. He was aware that the light he saw in the Spirit world was significant and took note of it. Because it was so vital, he ensured that he set aside time in his schedule each day to meditate in solitude and rekindle the fire within his heart. There were times when it was difficult, and he gained very little from it.

After he calmed down and made himself clear his thoughts, he had the sensation that he had been transported to the afterlife. His experiences had given him the confidence to talk to everyone about how wonderful those experiences were.

These extraordinary occurrences helped him further solidify the message that he needed to convey to his audience. The takeaway here is that each and every one of us possesses a special ability. A gift that was presented to them at the time of their birth or possibly even before their birth. A one-of-a-kind present that cannot be found anywhere else on the entire planet. A gift that can be of use to every single person on Earth. A gift the recipient may not fully appreciate for the rest of their life. And a gift that ought to be distributed among the people of the rest of the world.

***

He arrived on the shore shortly before dusk. His back was sore, his muscles hurt, and he had lost feeling in both of his legs. It took everything he had to pull the canoe to a higher spot on the beach where the waves wouldn't carry it away. After chewing on a piece of jerky, he wrapped himself in his blanket and dozed off while sitting on the beach.

When he opened his eyes, the sun was already up and beating down on his face. He grinned through strained eyes as he felt the warmth of the light and heat seeping through his blanket to him. While Qaletaqa was stretching, he reflected on how wonderful the sun was. How wonderful it was that it emitted light and heat for everyone to take pleasure in. Because the light from the sun was so powerful, it made him recall the brilliant illumination of the Spirit world he had previously explored.

He did so in a deliberate manner, eventually settling into a seated position with his legs crossed underneath him. He once more pulled his eyelids down, took a long, deep breath, and basked in the warmth of the magnificent sun. Because he was concentrating on the sunlight, he started to feel more relaxed. He emptied his thoughts and relaxed the muscles in his shoulders, neck, and back. As the tension in his shoulders eased, he also released the tightness in his arms, wrists, and fingers. He was able to detect a flow of energy emanating from the tips of his fingers. After that, he focused his attention on his back, his hips, his legs, and all the way down to the tips of his toes. After a while, Qaletaqa was able to unwind completely. His state of both mind and body was one of complete and utter bliss.

He basked in the tranquil, peaceful light for what seemed like hours as time passed slowly by. He had the impression that he was gliding through empty space and ascending toward the heavens. Even though Qaletaqa could see his body sitting on the beach below, he was not actually a part of that body. He had returned to a state of complete bliss and was moving very quickly. Qaletaqa was suddenly surrounded by a warm light and could see his Spirit guides consoling and protecting him as they stood all around him. He experienced an overwhelming sense of tranquility. The wolf, the bear, and the elk were all present at the gathering. They were all looking toward a brighter light, which was his father's vision, and they smiled with affection and warmth as they did so.

"Greetings, Qaletaqa."

"Hello, Father. Did I die again?"

"No, son," he said with a chuckle. "But it sure looks like you are mastering meditation quickly. I thought that you might."

"I feel so serene," Qaletaqa said. "It's nice to be back. Can I stay this time?"

"Soon enough, my son. Soon enough." His father chuckled. He looked down at his son and asked, "Do you know that you were chosen to see this glorious afterlife?"

"I'm not sure why, but I'm grateful," Qaletaqa admitted.

"What have you been doing while visiting the tribes you came from?" his father asked.

"Well, they seem to think I'm special in some way because I have shared with them the journey and all you shared with me. I keep telling them that I'm not special. I just had this unique encounter with all of you," Qaletaqa replied.

"Do you enjoy sharing what you learned in the Spirit world?"

"I think so, Father, but I'm not sure if they believe what I am imparting to be truths from your world or my made-up dreams."

His father chuckled again.

"There will always be non-believers, Qaletaqa. Don't worry about them. They may see the light someday or they may not. That is their journey. Your journey, however, is to keep sharing your experiences from the Spirit we have shared with you. This is your gift to share with the world," his father spoke.

As Qaletaqa contemplated his father's words and thought about sharing his knowledge with others, he smiled and felt entirely at peace. A warmth deep in his heart overwhelmed him. "I can and will share this gift with as many tribes as possible, Father." As Qaletaqa made this promise, the light dissolved, his father and Spirit guides were just a vivid memory, and he was seated back on the beach with the sound of surf crashing and pure white seagulls singing above.

Chapter 14
Spirit Teacher

The arrival of Qaletaqa was heralded by all as the Indian brave from the world of the Spirits, Kitche Manitou (Great Spirit) himself. Hunting parties and young braves who were sent out alone on vision quests spread the stories throughout the land, and they became more powerful with each retelling. Every community that lived in the great lakes region, including those in the upper and lower peninsulas, was aware of the Great Spirit. Some people believed it with all their hearts, while others just pretended to because they enjoyed the uplifting story that brought the members of the tribe together and gave them hope. Some people thought it was just crazy talk brought on by too much time spent puffing on their peace pipe. When Qaletaqa entered a tribal community and introduced himself to the members, regardless of the individual beliefs of the people there, everyone was stunned by his aura and went silent.

They could tell he was very different just by looking into his eyes. The skeptics eventually changed their minds after he shared the messages he had received from the Spirit world. Everyone yearned to believe that there was a Spirit world that awaited them once they had finished their work here on Earth and had successfully completed their lives. And right in front of them was living testimony. They needed the assistance of the great Kitche Manitou, Qaletaqa, who was present to explain the infinity of life.

He described his journey through the light and shared his experiences. He described the additional planes of existence as being breathtaking and assured them that there was no need for anyone to be concerned about life after this world. He imparted both the love of his father and the wisdom that he had received from a Spirit who called himself Jesus. He gave everyone the gift of understanding that they were a priceless treasure. Everyone brought their own unique contribution to the table, which they then shared with the rest of the world.

"You only need to find a quiet place, close your eyes, and open your mind to the light. The light will teach you everything you need and ultimately reveal the gift that is in you."

This was the message from Kitche Manitou, coming through Qaletaqa.

Qaletaqa shared his message to each village as he traveled, teaching tribe members, young and old, to believe in themselves. Many thought Qaletaqa could heal the sick, as well. But he told them he was sharing a message of life and had no healing powers.

Near the area now known as Little Traverse Bay, Qaletaqa encountered a village Chief, Chief Petoskey, struggling with his life. The tribe wanted Qaletaqa to save their Chief. He knew he was powerless to help and told them so.

But he then thought of Aki. If she were here, Aki would know what to do and perhaps could save him.

He told the other members of the tribe about Aki, a powerful medicine woman, and how she had nursed him back to health and how her knowledge of plants and herbs had helped save the lives of many people in her own village and the villages that surrounded it.

The tribespeople moved swiftly to send their most courageous warriors in their most maneuverable canoes to the island in the shape of a beaver, where they hoped to persuade a medicine woman named Aki to assist in the rescue of their leader.

When these men arrived at Aki's tribe, they were welcomed with open arms.

It didn't take much convincing when the braves told Aki that it was the great Spirit guide Qaletaqa who suggested they find her. When she learned that he was still in the village from where these braves came, she was more than willing to accompany them.

Aki knew this was her chance to venture off the small island and maybe help others. She met with her father.

"I must do this, Father," Aki explained. "Other tribes need my help as much as our tribe. I have trained our cousin in the ways of medicine and how to find the right herbs. She knows what to do and can help in my absence."

Chief Decomsie thought about her request. He was not happy about losing their medicine woman, not to mention his only daughter. But he also knew that young people need to venture out to find themselves and experience life.

"I will allow it on one condition," he began, giving Aki hope. "I want you to have some protection so our strongest warrior, Onadaga, will travel with you to make sure you are safe," Chief Decomsie stated. Aki's heart sank. This was the last thing she thought would happen.

"No, Father, that is not necessary," Aki refuted. "These braves that have come were sent here by the great Qaletaqa. You know he would never put me in harm's way, and he is on the distant shore awaiting my arrival and will certainly protect me there."

"That is the only way I will allow it," her father rebutted.

Aki had no choice in the matter. Her father's word was everything. She told herself that Onadaga's advances would be less likely while traveling in the big canoes with the other braves. And once they got to shore, Qaletaqa would be there to protect her.

She agreed to her father's conditions and began to pack her things. Although she was only going to heal the Chief of the other tribe, she was throwing more and more of her personal items in her bag, almost as if she was packing for a long journey.

***

It felt right, and she followed that feeling. She barely left any of her possessions in her hut, having tucked every last inch of her bag with the things that mattered to her.

The voyage lasted several days and took place over the same turbulent waters that Qaletaqa had experienced at the beginning of his journey. And just like Qaletaqa, Aki questioned whether or not she had arrived at the best choice. She had never traveled this far away from her island before, and while the experience was thrilling, it also made her nervous. When you were in the midst of the wave, you noticed that it was significantly larger. When you could hardly make out the outline of the ground on the horizon, solid ground was just a concept. She yearned for the security of solid ground beneath her feet. The braves finally paddled ashore landing on the soaring sand dune beaches of Little Traverse Bay, just as the sun set in the western sky.

***

Waiting on the beach, Qaletaqa led the group of tribesmen and helped drag the canoes ashore.

He held out his hand to help Aki from her canoe. His gentle touch was soft and warm and made her heart skip a beat. As she tried to stand, her legs gave out, and she fell into his strong arms. "It seems I have become unaccustomed to land," she said, flustered.

"Let me help you," Qaletaqa said. "Welcome to the mainland."

He lifted her into his arms and placed her gently on warm sand. He remembered her sweet smell from oils she worked with. He had missed this stirring scent.

Aki was surprised by his warmth and strong arms wrapped around her small body. It felt nice to her but a bit uncomfortable with all eyes on her, so she quickly separated and thanked him for his help.

"I'm so glad you could come to help," Qaletaqa said. "It's wonderful to see you."

Onadaga watched them closely. He quickly stepped between them.

"I am here to accompany Aki and make sure she is safe."

Qaletaqa eyed him. "Well, that's good. I want her to be safe, as well. You grab her belongings, and we'll leave immediately. The Chief is very ill."

Qaletaqa reached behind Aki to the small of her back and guided her gently in front of him toward the trail. They took off walking briskly.

Onadaga stood motionless and silent. The other braves quickly handed him Aki's belongings, and he seethed as he trailed the couple, aware that he was, at least for now, powerless.

He could not disrespect the great Qaletaqa in front of these braves. But he was determined. He would get his way.

The sick Chief's daughter cautiously approached them as they arrived at camp.

"Is this the great healer you speak of?"

The young woman dropped to her knees and thanked Aki for coming so far to help her father.

Aki gasped. Was she already known here?

"Qaletaqa, are you spreading tales about me? I told you I'm not that special."

"Yes, you are," he said. "You just don't realize it yet."

The tribe members ushered Qaletaqa and Aki to the Chief's hut. Aki grabbed her medicine bag from Onadaga and said, "You wait here."

Onadaga scowled.

After entering the hut, Aki placed her bag on the fur mats. She cast her gaze upon the Chief and performed an immediate evaluation of the Chief's health. She concluded that the best way to treat his condition was with a combination of herbs that she had successfully employed in the past. She dispatched members of the tribe in several different directions to search for the plants she required. After she had gathered everything, she made tea out of the herbs by boiling them and making the Chief drink it repeatedly for the next two days.

***

As they waited for Chief Petoskey to recover, Aki and Qaletaqa spent as much time together as they could. Qaletaqa tried to spend time with Aki alone, but Onadaga kept a close eye and never let them venture outside the tribal area by themselves. No matter where they were, he was there in the distance, constantly watching over them. It worried Qaletaqa. He knew what Onadaga had done to Aki in the past. It was probably tormenting her to know Onadaga was her guardian on this trip.

While waiting for Aki to finish checking on Chief Petosky, Qaletaqa was quietly meditating nearby. He was focusing on Aki and how he could help her when he felt a strong presence come up behind him. It seemed his inner Spirit was trying to tell him to turn around.

He opened his eyes to see Onadaga standing a few feet from him. He wasn't trying to hurt Qaletaqa, more to intimidate him with his large strong physique.

"I was hoping you would come to talk with me at some point," Qaletaqa said, standing up from his spot and dusting his legs off. Toe to toe, these men weren't that far off in height from one another. Onadaga definitely had more bulk to his upper body compared to Qaletaqa, but that didn't matter. They were still near the village, and people were walking near them, so Qaletaqa knew that Onadaga would not harm him.

"You and I both know that Aki is coming back with me to Beaver Island. Her father expects her to be back soon," Onadaga stated. Qaletaqa could see that the man in front of him was not one to be told no, so he would need to figure out a better way to tell him.

"I know that you care for Aki very much, and I'm sure her father does too. Don't you both want to see her happy? She has a great gift to share, and she should be sharing it with others," Qaletaqa explained.

"She needs to be back in her home. She has enough healing to do there," Onadaga rebutted. He took a step closer to Qaletaqa and crossed his arms over his chest to intimidate him.

"I don't understand why you are so possessive of her," Qaletaqa said.

"Because she belongs to me. So whatever you feel for her, just stop," Onadaga exclaimed.

Qaletaqa thought for a moment before responding, "It must be hard to constantly be angry and jealous of other people. Does that not drain your energy?"

"What are you talking about. There is nothing to be jealous of." Onadaga stepped closer.

"Okay, so you are not jealous, but you certainly are angry," Qaletaqa corrected himself. "That still must feel exhausting. Why do you choose to be so negative?"

Onadaga grew confused with the question. "Are you trying that Spiritual garbage on me?" he spat out. "You may have all these other people fooled, but you are nothing special. You're just a nobody."

"And yet Aki prefers to spend her time with me rather than you," Qaletaqa refuted. "So clearly, I am something to her." Onadaga let out a low growl and stepped closer to Qaletaqa.

"You let the anger ruin you, Onadaga," Qaletaqa started saying. "You allow it to consume you, and all you think about is yourself."

"Stop!" Onadaga yelled. Qaletaqa knew that he was hitting a sensitive spot with Onadaga and continued to push him.

"You think that your might is the only thing that defines you, and you lash out at anyone who doesn't bend to your will." Qaletaqa pressed on, "If you just allowed love into your heart, you would see that people aren't afraid of you; they are annoyed with you."

"Stop it!" Onadaga yelled louder, causing some villagers around them to take notice.

"If you allowed yourself to think of others and love them, people would want to be around you. You only think of yourself, and that is damaging your Spirit."

"I told you to STOP IT!" exclaimed Onadaga. He was about to lunge at Qaletaqa when he felt a hand pull on his shoulder.

"What is the meaning of this?" an elder asked. He had one of the strongest warriors holding Onadaga back while he stared down both men.

"I'm trying to help Onadaga with his anger," Qaletaqa admitted. Onadaga shrugged the man's hand off his shoulder and started walking away.

"I don't need his help!" exclaimed Onadaga. Once he was a safe distance away, the elder and the warrior looked back at Qaletaqa.

"I worry that this argument is not over between you two," the elder spoke softly. "I suggest you stay far away from him, and I will make sure our warriors keep an eye on him.

"I thank you for that," Qaletaqa said. "I only wish that you watch over Aki as well. He seems to be overprotective of her, and it's unwanted from her." The elder nodded in understanding.

"With our Chief on his way to recovering, I think it will almost be time for her to leave. Perhaps you can speak to her about that," the elder suggested, giving Qaletaqa a small smile. It was quite obvious how smitten Aki and Qaletaqa were with each other, and with Qaletaqa traveling to share his gift, why wouldn't Aki want to go with him to share hers?

Qaletaqa knew he wanted Aki to come with him; he just wondered how to convince her. And with Onadaga pressuring her to return home, he would need to speak to her sooner rather than later.

Qaletaqa was aware that the only way to get rid of Onadaga was for him to assume responsibility for her protection. So once Aki was done with her treatment of the Chief, Qaletaqa invited Aki to accompany him on his journey to other villages so that she could share her knowledge of medicinal plants and herbs to save lives.

Aki exhibited some trepidation. She had the desire to assist others. Because of how easily it came to her, she had no doubts about that. Why on Earth would Qaletaqa want her to accompany him on his further adventures? She could assist other tribes on her own. However, she was unable to travel by herself under any circumstances. She would require some form of protection.

She understood it was going to be difficult for her to convince Onadaga and the others to continue their journey without her. They had already started discussing the journey

175

back home. It's not like she wanted to go on the trip with Onadaga in the first place. That was not a secure move. Perhaps Qaletaqa had already seen this and was presenting her with various options.

She was by herself the next day and night, or at least as alone as she could be with Onadaga always close enough to hear her thoughts. She reflected on all her options and what was best for her. She spent the day and night alone. She contemplated going back to her island or continuing her journey so that she could help more people with her medicine. After giving it a lot of thought, coupled with the reality that she needed to get as far away from Onadaga as she could, she decided that she would remain here on the mainland for as long as she was required to assist others.

She planned to help Qaletaqa on his quest if he would allow her to.

Qaletaqa continued to enlighten the tribe elders and Chief with the wisdom he learned from the Spirit world. They could not get enough information from him, and he gladly shared everything he could.

One of the elders asked him, "Great Qaletaqa, you talk of the light from the Spirit world. We have this light within us constantly, and it is energy and power for us to harness and make us stronger. But as much as most of us try, we cannot keep this light in our minds. How do we keep the light all day and night to make us strong and find our gift to the world?"

"It is very difficult indeed to keep the light at the top of your awareness," Qaletaqa replied. "Fleeting thoughts keep our minds occupied. We must train our minds like how you train your bodies through exercise to become stronger. We can also train our minds to become stronger at keeping the Spirit light within us throughout the day. I work at training my mind in the morning when I arise, at midday before I sit down to a meal, and after the sun sets but before I sleep."

With that, he began to describe his own way of walking in the light.

"I begin by stretching all my limbs, my arms, my legs, my neck, even my toes and fingers. Then I find a quiet place to sit comfortably with my back straight. I close my eyes and concentrate on the light within me. I take a deep, slow breath in and hold it for a count of six, then I slowly exhale all the air in my body while I concentrate on the light within. I visualize the number sixty in my mind, illuminated by the light during the breath, in and out. I then take another slow breath, repeating what I did the first time, but I visualize the number fifty-nine. I repeat this activity until I reach zero. This will take at least an hour of time. Many thoughts will enter your mind during the activity, from hunting to family to what you want to eat and so on. Just peacefully let them go and return your focus to the light and count down the numbers to zero," Qaletaqa explained. Everyone around him murmured in acknowledgment, nodding and whispering to their neighbors.

Qaletaqa continued, "Some days, this will be easy for you. On other days it will be very difficult to maintain your concentration and keep the noise in your head away. It's okay. It takes time and practice, just like training your body for competition. Some days my concentration isn't there, but I still feel the benefit of the exercise, from increased energy in my body because I've been inhaling more air than normal to calm and peace from the light. Other times, when I'm really in tune with Spirit and can devote my full undivided attention to the light, I can visit the Spirit world again. In a meditative peace, the light from my body merges with the light of the Spirit world and transports me to other dimensions far from our own world."

"How long are you gone for?" a younger woman asked.

"Even if it seems like I've been away for days, almost no time has passed in this world. This is where you want to get to. Even a few quick minutes of meditation can give peace to your mind and soul. You should practice meditation every day as many times as you can. It is the lifeblood of your soul," Qaletaqa explained. The crowd murmured to each other again.

Qaletaqa caught Aki's eye from across the fire. She looked happy as she smiled at him. Maybe this was a good sign. Perhaps she was ready to take the leap and join him in educating others about their special gifts.

Chapter 15
Trouble

When Aki announced that the tribe's Chief was on the mend and would be fine, Onadaga declared that it was time for Aki to return with him to their tribe. Aki decided to turn around and head to a quieter place. She knew that Onadaga would follow her, and she didn't want to make a scene in front of everyone from the inevitable outburst that was about to happen.

"Qaletaqa and I have discussed other plans," Aki told him as she turned around. They were in a clearing out of earshot of the tribe but still within the boundaries. "He believes, and I agree, that I could be of much help to many tribes in the area. He is planning on traveling to as many tribes as he can before winter sets in to help them with their understanding of the Spirit, and I plan to help with medicine for tribes who have no medicine woman."

"No," Onadaga said. "You will come back with me. This is what the Chief expected. When your job is done, you will come home with me, your protector."

"I spoke with my father a great deal before I left and explained to him that this may be my Spirit calling. If people needed help in this area, I would stay and teach them all I knew about medicine and healing. I'm staying with Qaletaqa. He will protect me from now on," Aki stated firmly. Onadaga was upset and very angry. He then noticed how Qaletaqa was hovering around behind Aki, waiting to jump in if needed.

Onadaga could feel the rage bubbling up inside of him. These two were spending way too much time together, and now they had made plans behind his back.

No.

He would not allow this to happen. He would not lose her to this strange man.

Onadaga grabbed her by the wrist and began pulling her toward the canoes. Qaletaqa stepped in front of Onadaga.

"Let her go, Onadaga," Qaletaqa warned. "Aki has decided to stay and help. This is what the Spirits want."

"I don't care about the so-called Spirits that you think you know so well," Onadaga exclaimed. "You are a simple brave like me but have convinced others that you're some kind of God. You're nothing. Aki is coming with me."

"You don't have to do this, Onadaga," Qaletaqa pleaded. "You don't have to be so full of anger when things don't go your way."

"Is that what the Spirits told you?" Onadaga mocked. "Everyone needs to be happy together?"

"Yes, and maybe if you spent more time working on your own Spirit, you would understand that what you are doing is wrong. You can't treat Aki like a possession," Qaletaqa defended himself. "Your anger is why she doesn't want to be around you after what you did to her." Onadaga's eyes flared with red, and his cheeks puffed out in anger.

Qaletaqa grabbed the arm that was holding Aki. Onadaga let go of Aki and pulled a knife from his moccasin boot. As Aki ran from both of them, Onadaga swung the knife at Qaletaqa, catching him on his shoulder and chest.

Qaletaqa cried out in pain. Other warriors watching the interaction jumped in to save Qaletaqa from further injury.

Two jumped between Onadaga and the injured Qaletaqa. Quick with his knife, Onadaga slashed one brave across the cheek and was moving toward the other, then stopped. Onadaga looked down at the arrow stuck in his chest.

The Chief's son had fired an arrow as soon as he saw Qaletaqa in danger. He aimed for the torso, hoping to slow down or maim the raging brave with the knife. His arrow cut straight through Onadaga's chest.

As Onadaga fell, some of the tribesmen caught him and gently lowered him to the ground on his left side. Aki ran over and quickly withdrew her own knife, making fast work of cutting both ends of the arrow off, then gently pulling the protruding stick from his chest. As the blood flowed from his wound, coloring the ground and her clothing, Aki knew his injury was serious.

"Aki," Onadaga said, his voice weakening.

"Please relax, Onadaga. Everything will be okay," Aki tried to comfort him. He was losing blood fast, and his face began to pale.

He tried to tell her something but struggled to find the strength to speak. Aki bent down closer to his mouth to hear him.

"Please tell my father I'm sorry. And my mother that I love her." With that, he faded into unconsciousness.

Aki rubbed some plant oil on Onadaga's wounds after removing some of it from the bag in which she kept her medicines. Then, after collecting some leaves and mud, she made a bandage for his wounds, which she fastened with animal hide to staunch the flow of blood. She then focused on Qaletaqa as the new subject of her attention.

"Bandages are going to have to be applied to you as well," she stated. Before Qaletaqa could lose too much blood, she quickly stitched up his wound and bandaged it.

The other members of the tribe watched her in awe as she quickly responded to the danger and rescued the two braves. They were unanimous in their assessment that Aki was an experienced and skilled medicine woman. Aki gave the warriors who brought Onadaga to the mainland instructions that he needed rest for several months, and they followed those instructions. It wouldn't be long before he was back to his old self, but they couldn't let him move around or leave this tribal compound for any reason until he was fully recovered. Considering the severity of the wound, that could be anywhere from five to six new moons.

"Do not let him travel until then, or the wound could reopen inside him and kill him. Only time and rest could save Onadaga now," she instructed.

Aki felt bad about the incident but remembered the truths that she and Qaletaqa had written together. She needed to accept what happened just now and flow with life. She knew she had to move forward to fulfill her destiny. That would certainly be easier without Onadaga thwarting her every move.

That night, as she lay on her bed, she sought out the answers to what bothered her most. Was she truly doing the right thing and following her path? Was this incident a warning of what was to come?

She slowly calmed her breathing and began to meditate, focusing in on the Spirit and what answers it could bring her. She felt her body becoming weightless and a light surrounding her. She could see a bright light ahead. Her visions revealed other people surrounding her while she taught medicine and how to heal. She saw people hugging and crying with each other. She saw blood on the ground and a lifeless body.

She jolted awake. *What was that?* she thought. *Is that what Qaletaqa saw in the Spirit world?* It was very alarming and confusing at the same time. She looked beside her and saw that her medicine bag had fallen, and everything was scattered along the floor of the hut. She got up and went to clean things when she found her copy of Qaletaqa's eleven truths. Some liquid had spilled from one of the pots and splattered across the page, highlighting a certain truth. **Choose Happiness**

***

As soon as Qaletaqa was feeling well enough to travel, he and Aki continued their journey together northward from Petoskey to regions that Qaletaqa had never been to before and where the indigenous people eagerly ingested his message. While Aki tended to those who were ill and shared her own gift with those who were interested in learning how to heal, he instructed them on how to identify the Spiritual ability that was uniquely bestowed upon them. Warriors from the tribes that Qaletaqa and Aki visited were always one step ahead of them, telling nearby tribes that the Great Spirit was not far away. They had been cautioned to get ready. As a result of the preparations that had been made in advance, villagers eagerly anticipated their arrival and prepared lavish feasts and lively celebrations in their honor to meet them when they arrived. They had a good time at the receptions, but what really energized them was the chance to impart their wisdom to the welcoming tribes.

Qaletaqa became anxious about returning to his home in the south even though he had enjoyed sharing what information he could about the light. Instead of being known as Qaletaqa, a simple hunter, the indigenous communities that he had traveled to only knew him as the Spirit teacher.

How would people in his own village react to him? Regardless of the response, he would be happy to see his family, and he was looking forward to introducing Aki to his people. As soon as they arrived in a new tribe, she became the center of attention, and both men and women of the tribe gazed at her in awe because of her breathtaking beauty and her miraculous gift to cure the sick. Qaletaqa had no problem stepping aside and letting her take the initiative. As they traveled through Northern Michigan together, days turned into weeks, weeks turned into months, and months turned into a full year. Along the way, they stopped in various towns. Some communities consisted of only a half dozen families, while others were large fishing villages on the mainland close to the Straits of Mackinac, Saint Marys River, and even farther offshore to Bois Blanc Island, with more than one hundred people in total. They would stay for an entire month in larger villages, either to assist families in dealing with various illnesses or because every member simply desired to spend more time with the legendary Kitche Manitou.

Every village was excited that the great Kitche Manitou was actually there in their tribe. Nothing like this had ever happened. Chiefs would usher Qaletaqa to a large hut or teepee to learn from him about the Spirit world. Aki would be directed immediately to sick and ailing members.

A Kitche Manitou and a medicine woman visiting Mother Earth at the same time and in their village no less. This was a legend. This day would be spoken of through many generations.

Qaletaqa and Aki shared thoughts from time to time as they traveled to the next village, which was the only time they had alone. Qaletaqa felt closer and closer to Aki as months turned into a year, but he didn't think she had any feelings toward him. She went about her business only concerned with her patients' health. She was exhausted every night after administering her skills and comforting those in need. She loved to help and heal the sick.

Aki began to realize that Qaletaqa was right all along in telling her that this was her gift to the world. She would never want to stray from this path. She believed Qaletaqa felt the same way about sharing his wisdom from the heavens. They were a great team, a team with no worries other than which route to take as they ventured from one tribe to another, healing and teaching as they went. All their needs were met over and above what they could ever desire. Every tribe they visited was so grateful that they lavished Qaletaqa and Aki with food and drink and the most comfortable accommodations.

Their journey was so enjoyable and rewarding. Life was good.

Little did they know they were being hunted down like a lone deer pursued by a pack of hungry wolves.

Chapter 16
Tracked

The wounds that Onadaga sustained took a long time to heal. Because of this, he was constantly under stress, and it manifested itself in his irritability toward his tribemates as well as anyone else who tried to assist him or even come close to him. He continually ripped off his bandages complaining that he was ready to travel only to have them break open again. This continued for a number of months. Those who were closest to him made an effort to explain that Aki had left them specific instructions on how to assist him in achieving a full recovery, as well as the amount of time it would take to do so.

He had no interest in learning any of it. That made him even more agitated than he already was. Where exactly did she go? Why didn't she just take care of him herself and nurse him back to health instead of running off with Qaletaqa? He swore that he would track them down and make them both pay for their actions. His group of purported friends had reached their breaking point due to his never-ending complaining and outbursts of rage. Everyone eventually felt the wrath of this man, but in the end, he was the brave in command, so they had no choice but to submit to his authority.

***

Onadaga was prepared for his journey. He wanted to demonstrate this to the other braves in the group. After they had eaten corn and smoked meat, Onadaga grabbed Tomka, the brave who was the largest among them, wrestled him to the ground in front of the other warriors, and choked him until he tapped Onadaga on the shoulder as a sign that he was willing to give up the fight.

"We will leave tomorrow morning," he announced to the group.

As he rose from the ground, Tomka said, "We will provision the canoe tonight, then we will be ready to embark at first light."

"That won't be necessary," Onadaga said. "We are not going back to our island without Aki."

"But we have no idea where they are," Tomka murmured. "It's been several months since they left on their journey to help other tribes. They are too far away."

"That doesn't matter. We all know how to track down and kill the largest deer or bear. We can track them down, as well. It may take many moons, but I will not leave without our Chief's daughter," Onadaga exclaimed.

"I think the Chief knew she was going to stay for a while to help other tribes," complained Tomka. Onadaga slapped Tomka across the face harder than anyone had ever hit him before.

"No. Pack your provisions in hides you can carry easily because we need to travel as quick as the wind," stated Onadaga firmly.

There was no effort made to try to sway Onadaga's opinion in any way. They could tell that he was determined to follow through with his plan to locate Aki.

***

The following morning, all six ventured north in the same direction as Qaletaqa and Aki.

Village after village, they visited only to be pointed in another direction. Each stop was filled with stories of the legendary wisdom and healing of Qaletaqa and Aki. Week after week, month after month, they heard the same stories. Onadaga's rage increased with every story.

Tomka and the rest of the group were growing tired of tracking down Aki and Qaletaqa. It exhausted their bodies traveling to every island, looking for them, and it exhausted their minds from having to listen to Onadaga go on and on about how much he hated Qaletaqa.

At first, the warriors tried to persuade Onadaga that this wasn't worth it and that she would return to them one day. Onadaga would spew his anger and allow the cruelty inside of him to bring his fellow tribesmen down.

When his words weren't getting through to them, he became physical, punching and beating anyone who crossed him. The men were feeling defeated, and rather than try and stop Onadaga, they simply followed, barely speaking to him.

***

A Chief informed them just before the rise of the sixth moon on their journey that the great couple had left their tribe the day before.

Onadaga and his brothers were exhausted, but the thrill of knowing that they were getting so close to their target motivated Onadaga to continue traveling through the night. Before the sun rose, they crept stealthily around the next tribal compound they came across, close to the great Pigeon River. As the bravest of the strong departed for the morning hunt, they remained hidden.

Because of their unwavering bravery and tenacious strength, they were given the name Wolverine tribe. They located a secluded spot not far from the path that led from this village to the next one, and they knew that's where Qaletaqa and Aki would continue their journey. As soon as the sun peeked over the horizon, the once-dormant, lush conifer forest began to come to life.

With the sound of birds singing and squirrels foraging for pinecones and acorns on the ground, Onadaga and his men stood there in silence, waiting. Before they saw the people approaching, they heard soft footfalls on the trail. Onadaga's party emerged from the thick undergrowth just as Qaletaqa and Aki were taking their time entering the field of view.

Onadaga himself and another man grabbed Aki. Simultaneously, the other four grabbed Qaletaqa and threw him to the ground before he had any idea what was happening.

Aki screamed as Qaletaqa tried to wrestle his way free of the attackers. He was strong but outmatched by four braves holding him down.

Onadaga sneered at Qaletaqa. "I am here to return Aki to her village and a life with me. You will never interfere with her again."

"Why are you doing this, Onadaga? I have told you I don't want to be with you!" Aki screamed, trying to pull free from his grasp.

"If you cared for her, then you would respect her wishes. Let her go," Qaletaqa yelled. He struggled with the other braves, trying to escape their grasp.

"There is no point in arguing. I am doing what is best," Onadaga said. As he dragged Aki away, he gave orders to his tribemates, "Kill him."

Qaletaqa could hear Aki screaming as she was muscled away down the trail and out of view. He yelled out in both pain and frustration. He never thought in a million lifetimes that Onadaga would come down to this level. He must have tracked them down, searching through all the villages they had visited.

Now, he had Aki, and Qaletaqa was stuck here, about to be killed.

The four holding him hesitated. They glanced at each other, each understanding what the other was thinking. The blood of the Great Spirit Qaletaqa would be on their hands if they followed through with the commands of Onadaga. As they continued to hesitate, they heard the unmistakable sound of many footfalls running toward them. They were not alone.

***

The Wolverine tribe's hunting party heard the screams of Aki and the angry yells of Qaletaqa. They raced toward the commotion. Quickly surrounding Aki and her attackers, the hunting party demanded to know why these braves were dragging the great medicine woman away from Qaletaqa.

"She belongs back with her tribe and with me. I am her betrothed. She should not be here," Onadaga explained. Aki continued to try and break free from him.

"He's lying! I have never been betrothed to him. My father, the Chief, knows I am here with Qaletaqa," Aki tried to explain to the warriors.

"You are trying to take her against her will?" one of the tribe members asked.

Onadaga's answer was a swift attack of his knife into the neck of the closest brave, which caused him to release his tight hold on Aki. She still kept a knife concealed in her garments from the first attack. Aki dropped to the ground before Onadaga could grab hold of her again, then lashed out to the back of Onadaga's left thigh, slicing the main artery. The rest of the hunting party attacked efficiently and lethally. Onadaga collapsed with an arrow through his lung, and a hatchet sunk between his shoulder blades. His accomplice ran into the dense woods surrounding them.

***

Aki remained on the ground cowering from the attack, then realized these braves were here to save her. She screamed, "Get Qaletaqa! They are going to kill him!"

Two braves stayed with Aki as the others tore off down the trail in the direction where Aki was still pointing.

When Onadaga's men saw the braves stampeding toward them, they quickly released Qaletaqa and dispersed into the thick woods like rabbits fleeing a fox.

The braves helped Qaletaqa to his feet, asking if he was hurt in any way. Qaletaqa quickly responded that he was fine but expressed his grave concern for Aki. Just then, the other braves appeared with her safely between them. Aki ran into Qaletaqa's strong arms and melted into his body, sobbing with relief that he was unharmed. Qaletaqa held her tightly.

As their emotions ebbed, they released each other and moved apart, somewhat embarrassed by the stares of the braves surrounding them.

"Thank you," said Qaletaqa. "You saved our lives."

"This is our gift, to protect those around us," the warrior said.

***

They all returned to the spot where Onadaga lay in the dirt, unmoving.

"Why did these men attack you?" asked a brave.

Aki answered him. "These men are from my tribe. They travelled with me from the island we are from. They are good men sent to protect me, except for this one named Onadaga. This one always had anger in his heart and was very jealous of Qaletaqa, I believe. I will instruct his men to return his body to our island and explain these events. We are safe now, thanks to you."

She called out to the men who had fled, letting them know that she had no ill feelings toward them and that she needed their help to return Onadaga home.

They slowly appeared, one by one, shyly coming to her side.

"We are very sorry, Aki," said Tomka. "I don't believe any of us, in our hearts, wanted to hurt you or Qaletaqa. We were, of course, under Onadaga's direction, but we never understood his rage and the overwhelming quest to find you. Then when he told us to kill Qaletaqa, we knew he had gone too far. We never agreed to this."

"I know. Onadaga and I had a long history," Aki replied. "His ways were not something I approved of. I feel terrible that it came to this and that he has gone to the Spirit world. His family will be devastated. But I need you to tell them what transpired here and let my father know that I am safe with Qaletaqa and have more work to do on this mainland.

"I am sure he will be glad to hear that you are safe and following your destiny," Tomka replied.

"I am enjoying helping others and want to continue this work while they need me. I am teaching others how to heal the sick in every tribe I visit. Soon enough, I won't be as needed, and I will return to the island. Tell my father I promise this," Aki asked.

"We will do as you wish, Aki," spoke Tomka, looking down at the body of Onadaga.

The warriors offered to help bring the body back to the village so it could be wrapped and made easier to transport. The men humbly accepted, wanting to clean the body before bringing it back to their home.

As they lifted the body up and started walking away, Qaletaqa grabbed Aki's hand and pulled her back to wait with him. She turned to look at him and saw the sadness in his eyes.

"Do not let his death burden your Spirit, Aki. He took this too far and paid the price with his life," Qaletaqa reassured her. She nodded and felt a single tear fall down her cheek.

"I am not sad for me. I am sad for his family," Aki admitted. "I don't think they knew just how angry he was. How obsessed he was with me. I hope his family will forgive him."

Qaletaqa pondered that for a moment, "I hope they can too."

Chapter 17

Destiny

The assault left Qaletaqa and Aki in a state of shock. They were grateful to the brave and strong members of the Wolverine hunting party who had rescued them from certain death. Without them, there would have unquestionably been a disastrous result.

Neither of them was eager to continue their journey right away. They needed to restock on food and get some rest, so they followed the hunting party back to their village, where they were greeted with open arms once they arrived. After going through a terrifying experience, they were able to put their worries to rest and find some solace in the comfort of a hearty meal and friendly conversation.

They each went back to their wigwam and tried to fall asleep there. Neither of them could sleep because they kept thinking about the other and how close they came to never seeing each the other again, as well as the sense of loss that either of them would have experienced.

Aki was unable to pull herself away from obsessive thoughts of Onadaga's passing. It was painful for her to witness someone she had spent her childhood with deteriorate into such a violent person that he needed to be taken down. Even though he was awful to everyone, especially her, he was still a person at his core. This was especially true for her. She couldn't help but feel relieved that she wouldn't be present when his body was brought back to their tribe. She could only try to fathom how devastated his parents would be to learn that he had passed away.

She also reflected on her relationship with her father. He was aware of how she felt and that she thought it was necessary to travel with Qaletaqa on this journey. Her father held the man in high regard and was confident that he would do anything in his power to ensure the safety of his daughter. That theory was proven today.

This was something that was very important to her, and because he loved and respected her so much, he understood that this would bring her a great deal of joy. And that was the only thing he ever desired for her.

Because he was primarily concerned about Aki, Qaletaqa had trouble falling or staying asleep. What they saw today was probably traumatic for her, and despite the fact that she was a strong woman, she probably felt sad as a result of what they saw.

Qaletaqa felt sad.

He had put a lot of stock in the idea that he would be able to save Onadaga. He merely desired to connect with him, but his attempts were pointless. Qaletaqa entered a state of meditation and inquired of the Spirits regarding the inability to assist Onadaga. He did not receive a response to his question, but a wave of peace washed over him as he realized that Aki would be in a less dangerous situation now that Onadaga was no longer a threat to her.

Both eventually, and gratefully, succumbed to sleep.

They made the decision to extend their stay by one day so that they could assist the Wolverine tribe with some minor tasks, such as foraging for necessary herbs that Aki knew how to find quickly. They took pleasure in making light conversation while trying to relax and regain a sense of normalcy.

The next day, they awoke feeling revitalized and prepared to continue their journey. They hugged each other and said their goodbyes to the Wolverine tribe, promising to return.

***

The trek in a westerly direction took them through a magnificent hemlock forest as well as some cool spring-fed lakes, where they were able to refill their water skins. Aki began to realize that the lack of conversation was about much more than just thoughts of the attack that occurred two days ago. From the way that he walked so slowly and quietly, she was able to deduce that he was anxious about the prospect of going back home.

During the days they spent traveling, Aki constantly urged them to stop moving and set up camp around dusk. She could have continued for a while longer, but she was aware that she needed to assist Qaletaqa in pausing for a while before moving closer to his tribe.

During a particularly long and taxing day spent traveling and thinking in solitude, Aki realized that he needed something more than just time.

She shielded them from the brisk, swirling winds by selecting a moss-covered, verdant plateau that was surrounded on two sides by sheer rock walls. As they were preparing to sleep, they came to the realization that they had never been left alone, away from the watchful eyes of other members of their tribe. They gratefully sank to the ground and covered themselves in luxurious animal skins. Above them, a canopy of a million stars unfolded in front of them. They were both worn out, so they decided to simply take in the silence.

Neither one of them was prepared for the sudden onset of the night's chill, given that they were without the protection of a covered hut to keep them warm. As Aki started to shiver, the thought came to her head, *this is ridiculous.*

The combination of two bodies would almost certainly produce a higher temperature. As Qaletaqa watched Aki move closer to him, he was thinking the same thing.

There was no reason to be embarrassed. The coming together of the two was the most natural thing that could have ever happened.

When their bodies came closer together, a warmth that was more than just physical engulfed them. Because their coming together was so natural, it gave the impression that this was the position in which they were intended to remain permanently.

Aki buried her icy nose in the warm neck of her companion. She was taken aback when she felt him kiss her on the forehead. She brought her lips up to his, and he kissed her full lips gently at first, and then he encircled her mouth with all the passion that he had stifled for such a very long time. Both parties had fantasized about being able to embrace one another, but nothing could have prepared them for the reality of the situation. They were completely overcome by their feelings when they realized that this was indeed their destined path.

Holding each other while sobbing, crying, and laughing at themselves for several hours after the event was something that, as far as they were concerned, could have continued indefinitely. No one could ever pull them apart. They slept until the morning hours, wrapped in each other's arms and embracing one another.

Chapter 18
Okwi

Okwi felt like her heart had been torn out of her body.

She toiled longer each day inside the family wigwam where she lived, fluffing Qaletaqa's bed and replacing cedar bows underneath the plush furs in order to keep it clean and presentable for his arrival. However, she was aware, on some level, that it had been far too long. Her Qaletaqa was most likely another victim of the great forest, a forest that provided them with the food and shelter they required but also contained a great deal of peril in the form of many kinds of threats. An unexpected natural disaster, such as a violent storm or an encounter with a wild animal, could take the life of a loved one. After losing her husband in the same treacherous forest so many years ago, Okwi knew all too well what she was up against.

Her unwavering faith in the Spirits who guided and watched over them was the only thing that brought her peace. She prayed that the same merciful Spirits would be bestowed upon both her husband and her son. She had a dream that her loved ones were all together in the Spirit world and that they were taking care of each other and having a wonderful life together.

This day felt different. She was on her last thread of hope and, after this, would give up on believing that her son would come home. She sat on Qaletaqa's bed, ready to move on with her life. She bowed her head and cupped her face in her hands.

I miss you both so much. I know I have responsibilities here taking care of our family. I'll feed and protect them with my life. I just hope my life mission here is a short one because I yearn to be with you both again. I miss your embrace, my love. And I miss your smile, Qaletaqa. I know I'll be with you both soon enough, and I'll try to be patient, but my heart hurts every hour of the day. Please give me a sign you are both well. I need to know.

She worked hard to keep a pleasant demeanor with her other children, as well as with the rest of her family and her friends. She encouraged her children to have hope, made sure everything was kept in order, and prepared meals for them. The hope was that Qaletaqa would be taken care of properly. The expectation was that the great Spirits were guarding him at all times. They held onto the hope that their brother would come back to them one day. We held out hope that some of the other young men from our tribe would make it back home safely.

Once a month, a young and courageous person would return from their own journey to discover who they were. The members of the tribe would start cheering and hugging each other for a very long time. All the members of the tribe, including the children, listened raptly as tales were told about their journey. Naturally, Okwi kept pinning her hopes and saying her prayers on the possibility that her Qaletaqa would one day come back to her. Despite having her hopes dashed on a regular basis, she would still muster the strength to put on a cheery smile and greet the returning young men.

She buried her feelings by keeping herself busy, but at some point, during each day, she would make an effort to go down to the shoreline and relive the moment that Qaletaqa left. She would get down on her knees in the powdery sand beneath the towering pines that guarded the shoreline and pray for him to come back. Here, by herself, she was able to cry her heart out without being judged. Even now, after two very long years of being without her son, she still cried her heart out in anguish every time she thought of him.

Chapter 19

Home

As they neared Qaletaqa's home, Aki again felt his nervous tension, the same apprehension she sensed during those wordless moments on their travels.

She took his hand, looked up at him, and reassured him.

"Everything will be fine, Qaletaqa," she said. "Not only are you a great teacher now, but your tribe loves and misses you. They will love to have you home."

Qaletaqa drew in a deep breath and relaxed his shoulders. She knew the perfect thing to say to help him feel strong and more comfortable in tense situations.

I love this girl, he thought.

They continued hand in hand, to the village.

***

The days, months, and years that had passed over the course of Qaletaqa's mother's lifetime had turned into a routine. She kept herself occupied by fashioning furs for her sons and daughters as well as preparing meals using wild game that her children brought to her at home. Because she missed her son Qaletaqa so much, there were times when she could barely get through the day without breaking down in tears. When she allowed herself to contemplate the possibility that her son might be hurt or killed, her heart broke. Despite her resilience and her unwavering belief that he would eventually come back to her, she was all too familiar with the perils of the northern woods and the harm that they could have caused to her Qaletaqa.

On this day, her thoughts were dissuaded from continuing by a group of adolescents who were discussing the Kitche Manitou.

"He is near this area. He may even appear here one night out of the evening mist," said one of the young men, laughingly jesting the girls in his audience.

She, like so many other tribespeople, heard the stories of some great Spirit teacher who had descended to this Earth to help tribesmen everywhere.

A real Kitche Manitou here in our land, she thought. *I'll believe it when I see it for myself.*

***

Qaletaqa had been gone for a total of three years at this point. The crops flourished and were collected for harvest on three separate occasions. With each harvest came the realization that another winter was drawing near, and Qaletaqa would not be returning for yet another year. The majority of Okwi's leisure time was spent meandering along the shore, hoping against hope that she would see a canoe approaching from the distance, in which her son would be paddling.

Since Qaletaqa left the village at the age of eighteen, she had seen a lot of other brave young people leave the community. The difference was that each of these young warriors came back from their adventures with incredible tales of daring hunts, foreign lands, and mysterious peoples.

These courageous individuals also brought back tales about a great Spirit teacher they had heard about from members of other tribes. She paid only a passing interest in what was being said. She believed that Spirits were wonderful, but what she really wanted was her son.

When each young brave returned, a celebration was held to mark their transition into manhood. This occurred in conjunction with their return.

She behaved appropriately and attended the soirees, where she complimented each brave participant. However, the celebrations tore at her heart, each one doing a little more damage as the days went by without any sign of her son.

Other families urged her to maintain an optimistic outlook regarding Qaletaqa's imminent return. But after three arduous years, they were all aware that there was a strong possibility that he would never come back. In contrast to the fables and myths that were eventually debunked, the legends of the great Kitche Manitou continued to be passed down. She presumed that, in the course of time, this story, along with the others, would also be lost to the whispering winds. On the other hand, it appeared that, almost daily, someone knew that the great Spirit teacher was getting closer. That he had been spotted in a community that was not too far away. When Qaletaqa's mother was tending to her fire on a cool October evening just after dusk, she heard a commotion in the middle of the village and immediately turned her attention there. The Chief was giving orders to everyone in the village to get the settlement ready.

She dispatched her oldest son to investigate the commotion and find out what it was all about. He returned with his eyes wide open. As he struggled to catch his breath, he informed his mother that the legendary Kitche Manitou was going to visit their community.

She remained a disbeliever.

"The old fools believe that. You tell me when this Spirit arrives, if ever. I'll continue with my fire in the meantime, and you go fetch more wood. We'll need it tonight. It's getting cold."

"Mom," her son said, exasperated. "It's true. The Chief is having everyone ready for a celebration."

"You never mind, and go get that wood."

She looked out over all the activity in every corner of the village and shook her head. *How could everyone be that gullible?* she thought.

***

Someone who had watched him leave the harbor three years earlier might not have recognized him at first glance as he approached. Over the course of time, Qaletaqa had developed. He kept getting taller, and his hair was now at an extremely impressive length. He carried himself as the most impressive Chief in the tribe because he wore a full headdress made of eagle feathers. Each of the indigenous communities that he encountered adorned the headdress with feathers as a sign of their gratitude and respect. Any tribe would have been proud to own an eagle's tail feathers because of their rarity and value. This feather was revered for its status as the mighty warrior of the heavens. Eagle feathers were carefully stored away for use in important ceremonies. They were rarely, if ever, given away to anyone. Yet each tribe desired for Qaletaqa to depart with their most prized possessions.

Additionally, the furs that he wore were gifts. They were quite dissimilar to the furs of his own tribe, which he had taken with him when he left. The length and abundance of the furs that were bestowed upon him rivaled those bestowed upon the most illustrious Chiefs in the region.

When Qaletaqa and Aki arrived at his home, even though it seemed like a lifetime ago, they were greeted with the same fanfare as they had been elsewhere. Everyone, except for the village Chief, dropped to their hands and knees as they were led through the village by several braves.

Nobody was able to recognize him.

Standing before Qaletaqa with his arms outstretched and his head bowed in gratitude, the Chief thanked the great Spirit teacher for bestowing his presence on the village.

As the Spirit teacher passed by the Chief, he quickly acknowledged his presence and thanked him for his assistance. The Chief was taken aback by the succinct response, as it seemed as though he had more important things on his mind. But he'd never met a Spirit. He thought perhaps that was just how they acted in general.

But even with just those few words, he had the impression that he had heard that voice before.

When the great Spirit teacher arrived in the village, Qaletaqa's mother was emerging from her teepee to greet him. Even from one hundred feet, she was taken aback by the legendary figure's breathtaking appearance. He was physically imposing, a muscular and decorated soldier who was accompanied by a woman who was equally as beautiful.

Now more than ever, she had no choice but to accept the fact that Kitche Manitou existed, at least in the physical sense. She followed the example of the other members of the tribe and knelt in the position of worship just outside the entrance to her hut.

To her shock, the Spirit teacher and his companion walked directly in her direction.

They were very close now. It took all her will to focus on the Earth below her and not look at the Spirit. *Why is he so close to me?* she thought. *Why did he stop in front of me?*

"Hello, Mother," said Qaletaqa. "I have missed you so very much."

That voice….was so familiar. Did he just call her "Mother"? What was happening? The voice prompted her to take a closer look, and she gasped. It was her Qaletaqa. She got up from the ground and embraced him in a smothering hug.

"Qaletaqa," she cried. "It's Qaletaqa! You're home. Everyone, it's Qaletaqa."

His siblings disregarded the respectful worship position immediately, pulling themselves to their feet. They all joined in the family embrace, a circular mewling of homecoming and happiness.

The rest of the tribe looked on with confusion: This was Qaletaqa, the brave who had been brought up among them? Was he the great Kitche Manitou?

As shock turned into the realization that their lost brave Qaletaqa had become the great Spirit teacher, the rest of the tribe joined in the celebration with Qaletaqa and his family.

***

The Chief strolled into the frenzied huddle of his tribe to get a better look at the great Spirit teacher, or, as they knew him all his life, Qaletaqa. As the rest of the tribe realized that their Chief was in the mix, they quieted their elation to allow him to speak.

"Qaletaqa, how did this come to be that you are a great Spirit now?"

"I have a lot to share with all of you," Qaletaqa responded. "It was a real journey. I never thought that anything would have come from it, but I saw things and felt things I will never forget."

"You have been gone for several years; what have you been doing through all this time?" the Chief asked. Qaletaqa looked over at Aki and then smiled back at the Chief.

"I was taught important lessons on my journey, and I was given a gift to share with others," Qaletaqa explained. "I have spent the past few harvests traveling with my companion, Aki. Together, I have taught the truths of the Spirit world, and Aki has used her gift as a medicine woman to teach tribes how to heal themselves."

"A medicine woman?" the crowd murmured. The Chief was equally as shocked to hear of such a woman sharing her gift with others.

"We are honored to have you home and would be grateful to listen to the story of both of your journeys," the Chief spoke.

"We wish to stay for the winter if you will have us," Aki asked. The villagers waited for the Chief to speak, hoping he would allow them to stay so they could hear his stories and teachings.

"You don't even need to ask. This is your home, Qaletaqa, and now yours, Aki," the Chief replied. "You stay for as long as you like."

Okwi hugged her son even tighter, knowing that he would be here with her for at least the next few months. While he had stories to tell their tribe, she was just happy to know that he would be here with them and that he was okay.

Epilogue

The celebration went deep into the night as Qaletaqa answered the barrage of questions from family and friends. Chief Owosso finally stepped in and asked everyone to give Qaletaqa and Aki some time to rest.

"You will all have plenty of time to ask questions after sunrise tomorrow," the Chief said. The tribe was sullen from having to step away, but they wanted to respect the Great Manitou by allowing him to rest. Since he would be staying for the winter, they had plenty of time to ask him questions.

***

Before Qaletaqa could retire for the night, he knew he had to share an important part of his adventure with his mother. Qaletaqa and Aki followed her into her wigwam, where Okwi quickly threw together a large basket of berries, slices of bread, and dried meats.

"Mother, come sit with us. You don't have to feed us. We are just fine. And I have much to tell you," Qaletaqa reassured her.

"Don't be silly. You have been traveling long and need to eat to keep your strength." She laughed, still not quite believing her son was with her again.

As they settled into the warm furs around the fire pit in the middle of the wigwam, Qaletaqa smiled warmly at his mother. He missed her as much as she missed him.

He knew what he wanted to tell her, but he feared how she would react to the news. It was not something she was expecting to hear, so he could only assume that she would have a lot of questions and maybe even get upset.

"I saw Father," Qaletaqa stated. He watched his mother as she processed his words. Her smile slowly fell, and her face drained of all its color.

"What are you talking about, Qaletaqa? Your father was killed many years ago. I prepared his stiff body myself for the ceremonial fire that sent him to the Spirit world," Okwi replied. She was concerned and suddenly felt sick to her stomach. This wasn't possible. There was no way he could have seen his father.

"I know, Mother." Qaletaqa quickly consoled his mother, who looked like she was starting to panic. "I was with Father in the Spirit world during my adventure. I'll tell you more about all of that tomorrow. For now, Father wants you to know that he misses you terribly, but he is well. He is living a glorious life on another plane of existence that you will travel to someday and be reunited with him. He is anxious to be with you again but knows you are needed here on Earth still," Qaletaqa explained. He grabbed his mother's hand in comfort and reassurance.

"He came to you in the Spirit world?" Okwi asked, confused. "I don't understand how this is possible."

"I will tell you every detail tomorrow, I promise," Qaletaqa said. "I need you to trust me right now, though. I saw my father and talked with him. He wanted me to pass along that message as soon as I saw you."

"Oh, Qaletaqa. You don't know how much my heart is lifted by your words." Okwi began to sob, allowing her heart to fill with the love she felt for both her son and her husband.

"Father knows you miss him terribly and how much your heart aches. He wants you to know that everything is wonderful in the Spirit world and that you will both be together again. He wants you to live without pain in your heart."

Qaletaqa continued, "He said to tell you to live each day with love for everyone around you and not to worry about him or anyone else who has ventured to the next plane of existence, for it is a perfect place with more abundance and love than you could ever imagine."

"I think I can do that," Okwi replied, wiping the tears that fell from her eyes. "I am just so happy that you are back, and I have you here with us again. I love you, Qaletaqa."

"I love you too, Mother. We'll talk more tomorrow." Qaletaqa and Aki got up and went to leave the wigwam before Okwi spoke quietly.

"Is this all real? Or am I dreaming?"

"I am here, Mother. This is real," he answered. She nodded her head in understanding and allowed the two to find their lodging for the night.

***

Qaletaqa and Aki were awakened by the sounds of the village coming to life for the day. To avoid being bombarded with questions, Qaletaqa snuck Aki out the back of their hut, down a soft earthen trail through a majestic hemlock forest, to his favorite beach on the shores of Pine Lake. They swam together, enjoying the time alone and savoring the refreshing water. They felt as if they had been a couple forever.

Upon their return to the village, Chief Owosso called the members of the tribe to gather at the small amphitheater and fire pit to listen to Qaletaqa and Aki tell their adventures with more detail than had been allowed the night before.

Before a majestic campfire, Qaletaqa began with the storm that nearly took his life.

"The waves were tall and kept pushing me over. I felt this feeling of dread that I may drown. I suddenly felt darkness surround me, and I thought I must be dead." The crowd gasped as they were astonished that someone could survive such an ordeal. Huge waves in open water was certainly a death sentence.

"But then, I was flying through glorious light. It was everything. I was light, and I was surrounded by light, and I saw Earth just getting farther and farther away," Qaletaqa explained.

"How were you light?" someone asked from the crowd. Qaletaqa smiled.

"This light was my first great lesson from the Spirit world," Qaletaqa continued. "The light of the Spirit world has everything we need to help us and teach us the Earth lessons we are here to learn. Everyone, close your eyes and concentrate on a spot just above your eyes in the middle of your forehead. Envision bright light coming from the heavens into your mind and surrounding you with warmth. If you take time every day to practice seeing and feeling this nourishing light, you will receive everything you need for your life here on Earth.

"How does the light help us in our lives?" Chief Owosso asked.

"The light is your Spirit guide to help you find your way and answer any questions you have. This light will eventually show you the special gift you have to share with this world," Qaletaqa replied. "We all have a gift, and the sooner you realize what your gift is, the sooner you will enjoy your life here on Earth. It is your Spirit gift. I believe my gift is sharing this exact message with everyone." The crowd murmured to one another. This was an interesting revelation. To have a gift special to each one of us and be able to live happily with that gift seemed intriguing.

"Aki has a beautiful gift of healing people that she learned from her mother, her grandmother, and even the Spirit of her great-grandmother. She is one of the lucky ones that was shown her gift at a very young age. Now she is a great medicine woman and has healed ailing members of tribes across this northern territory. This is her Spirit gift." Qaletaqa gestured to Aki, who was sitting beside him.

"Some of us know the gift we have been given and begin using it immediately. Others take many years to figure out their gift. Then there are some who never figure out their gift before their Earth bodies die and return to the Spirit world," Qaletaqa explained.

"Why do we need to know our gift?" a young boy asked.

"It's so important to learn your gift because it makes your life important and graceful. Those who know their special gift and use it daily to help humanity breeze through life effortlessly helping people," Qaletaqa said. The child seemed to understand and nodded his head.

"When you close your eyes and concentrate on nothing but your Spirit light, this is called meditation. If you meditate daily for at least an hour, you will find your Spirit gift if you haven't already and bring peace and happiness to yourself and those around you. Even a few minutes of meditation will help calm you and give you energy, but longer periods will be much more beneficial. Meditation will give you peace and allow you to flow through life without fear and concern." Qaletaqa looked out at the crowd of people and watched them take in this information. It was a lot to explain to them, but it was the most important thing he could teach them.

"There is also tremendous knowledge stored in the light. Our ancestors who have transitioned into the Spirit world can share knowledge with us through the light. Simply ask them. You may not get the answer immediately, but soon you will. Just keep going back to the light," Qaletaqa stated.

"We can speak to our ancestors? Those we have lost to the Spirit world?" another tribesman shouted.

"The light connects you with everything on the planet, from other humans to trees and flowers and even the sand that you walk on. Therefore, it is so important to love everyone and everything. Set your ego aside and help those in need because life is short. We all pass on to the next plane of existence sooner or later, so live with grace, peace, and lightness. Avoid anger and frustration. Choose happiness."

As Qaletaqa explained his truths and what he learned from the Spirit world, he watched the crowd of his fellow tribe take in and understand what he was saying. He knew that it was a lot of information and that maybe some things just seemed outlandish and odd. But he also knew that what he was saying was true and that it worked. He followed these truths, as did Aki, and their lives were meaningful. They both had their Spirit gifts and shared those gifts with those around them.

It was more fulfilling than any fight or hunt he had ever done. He felt whole and filled with purpose. Once he had explained his truths, he began breaking it down and discussing how to meditate properly.

"Breathing deeply throughout the day can help bring peace and happiness. We all breathe automatically, of course, but these breaths are shallow. When you concentrate on deep breathing, like when you're meditating, it relaxes your body completely. If you concentrate on breathing deeply every moment of the day, it will soon become a habit, a habit which will bring peace and health to you far above what you are experiencing now." Qaletaqa could see that many tribespeople began to slow their breathing. It was amazing to watch as people took in his teachings and then started to complete them in front of him. Regulating and slowing breathing was important to get into the right headspace, and these people were very willing to try it.

"Controlling your breath will allow you to control your life and help you grow and live like the great hemlock tree. The hemlock puts down strong roots over time and grows slowly to great heights, becoming the sturdiest tree in the forest. Other trees in the forest grow faster and taller but end up with a shallow root structure and are easily blown down in the first storm.

You must grow and live life like the hemlock. Slowly build a strong base, then continue reaching for the stars. This way, when setbacks happen in life—and they will—you are prepared to weather any storm."

Aki watched as Qaletaqa taught the crowd of people, and it brought her such great joy to observe this. He truly had a way with words and explained things so well to others. This was truly his gift to the world. He was amazing.

"Many of us try to accomplish too much too fast. Trying this, trying that, trying to be good at everything but never really mastering what you are here to learn and give to the world. Think about your Spirit gift and advance toward learning and sharing that gift and nothing else. Sharing your gift will give you all the peace and recognition in life you want and deserve."

Okwi wanted to cry as she saw her tribe listening intently to what her son was teaching. He had captivated this crowd with his joy and passion. She was extremely proud of the man that he had become, and she knew that his father was watching over him just as proudly.

"Lastly, and more important than all the rest, is to live with love in your heart toward everyone and everything. Loving life and loving everyone and everything in this world will give back to you everything that's important." Qaletaqa looked over at Aki and gave her a loving smile. She returned the gesture, feeling all the love in her heart and his with this look of adoration.

"Sharing love will generate peace in your soul. Sharing love will generate love from others back to you. Loving everyone will strengthen your own roots and give you a solid foundation, so when that setback happens, your family and friends will rally around you, protect you, and help you through any storm. When you give love, it always returns to you when you need it most." The crowd cheered with admiration and excitement. They wanted to learn more and practice along with Qaletaqa. They wanted the life he described to them. They wanted purpose and love in their lives.

The celebration continued into the night. Everyone was excited that Qaletaqa was the legend every tribe was talking about. The Qaletaqa from their tribe was the great Kitche Manitou.

He had returned a the beautiful medicine woman, Aki, who was already helping the sick and ailing in their small tribe. There were quite a few interested in learning more about healing, as they had never had someone like her in their tribe before. They watched patiently and inquisitively as she found the correct herbs and tonics. She taught them with patience and kindness and was a pleasant person to be around. As Chief Owosso watched his tribe prosper at their new beginning, he couldn't help but exclaim, "What a miracle."

***

The following morning, Qaletaqa and Aki quietly slipped off to Qaletaqa's favorite spot high up on the sand dunes above the inland lake surrounded by towering hemlock trees.

Qaletaqa brought dried meats and fruit so they could be alone for a while and contemplate everything that had happened over the last several months. A large animal's skin kept them warm. As they gazed at the lake, the trees, and the horizon, Qaletaqa spoke up. He began with a recitation of his journey into the Spirit world, a story she had heard before and never tired of.

Only this time, he had more to tell.
"I speak of the beautiful woman I met in the Spirit world," Qaletaqa said. Ever since you started taking care of me three years ago, I knew you were familiar to me. At first, I thought it was because you cared for me so well. But as time went on, I was sure that I knew you from somewhere. I couldn't figure it out until the last couple of days, but then it dawned on me that

you are the Spirit I met on the third plane during my travels through the Spirit world.

"I saw your Spirit in the Spirit world," Qaletaqa admitted to Aki as they stared into each other's eyes.

"How is that possible?" Aki asked.

"You must have been sleeping. When you sleep, your Spirit visits the Spirit world to recharge, and you came to me in one of the planes," Qaletaqa explained. Qaletaqa remembered their exact moment together.

A woman of unparalleled beauty crossed the river toward him, emerging from waist-deep water. Her body was small but muscular as she slid effortlessly through the rapid river. She had long dark hair, pale caramel skin, and dark eyes that entranced him with curiosity as she smiled warmly.

It was Aki all along.

"I feel like I have loved you forever," he had admitted to the woman.

"You have," she replied. *"Qaletaqa, we've been in love for thousands of years. You don't remember since you're on another earthly adventure and haven't found me yet. You will, however. I believe in you."*

Qaletaqa believed her claims to be valid. They had a magnetic draw to one another and always found each other in each generation.

"You and I have been destined together for thousands of years," Qaletaqa told her, his voice wavering at the pure emotion he was feeling.

"We always find each other," Aki stated.

"We always find each other," Qaletaqa repeated

It made so much sense to her. She had, as well, felt an indescribable bond with him.

"You are familiar to me too, Qaletaqa. We are so comfortable with each other, and we belong together. All the while growing up on the small island with my tribe, I felt in my heart that I would meet someone special. Someone who could understand my need to heal others and respect that part of me. Someone who would love me forever. I don't know the Spirit world that you speak of, but I'm glad you found me because I have the same feelings for you. I love you, Qaletaqa."

"And I love you, Aki."

Qaletaqa jumped to his feet and walked away, holding a finger to her that said, "Please wait for a second." She laughed as she patiently waited for him to return.

He returned within minutes with a bouquet of purple wildflowers. He pressed the bouquet to his heart, then handed it to her.

Wordlessly, they embraced. Together, they saw infinity, a life to be lived on all planes. Their destiny was clear—teaching, learning, and healing, of course.

What propelled them, though, with the softest, safest of confidence, was their combined love that created a stirring, Spiritual bond. Soon they would realize with delight that they had conceived a new soul. A soul they created together. A soul that would change the world.

Together, they descended the dunes hand in hand, ready to help all humanity.

Appendix
Eleven Truths

We Are Light

We are nothing more than light. Light is our source of energy. Our source is light. Light is our link to the world beyond. Light is everything, and when we focus internally, we only see the light. We can travel to other worlds by following the light. Worlds from which we came before our time on Earth. Worlds from which we derive our life energy. When we sleep, we replenish our daily energy from this light source.

Consider it this way. You sleep when you are exhausted and unable to continue. When you awake, you feel revitalized and energized. This happens every day.

Where does this renewed vigor come from? You were sleeping the entire time. How does sleep provide energy?

This energy comes from your source, the light. In dreamless sleep, the source replenishes your energy. So, when you sleep well, your light—or Spirit—returns to the source, which replenishes your energy.

What other explanation could there be? You get some energy from food and water and some from sunlight, but the majority of your energy comes directly from the source while you're sleeping.

During quiet, deep meditation, you can connect directly with this light energy whenever you want.

We Are All Connected
Every living thing is part of the same energy source.

You are Spiritually connected to your family, friends, tribal members, neighboring tribes, and people across the world. You are Spiritually connected to your pets and other animals, every species, flower, plant, and tree. We are all an intimate part of each other through Source energy, the light. We are here to love everything and everyone.

We Are More Than Our Ego
You identify every day with the person you see. Yet the face and body you recognize every day are not you. It's simply your ego or how you perceive yourself. You want to rise above your ego self.

Consider yourself as only light energy currently having a human experience. This is accomplished by living in the present. Forget about what happened to you yesterday, which shaped your ego. Forget about and stop worrying about the future, which you cannot change. Live today, only today, only this minute. Because that's all there really is.

Accept What Happened, Then Strive to Change
Accept what has happened to you or your loved ones completely, but always strive to change and improve.

What has happened to you cannot be changed because it was predestined to happen for one reason or another in your life. Because you can't change it, let it go and get on with your life. We have no idea why things happen the way they do. Why did a loved one become ill or die? What happened to cause us to lose everything financially? Why did we become wealthy? Why do we have to deal with such a crippling disease? What is the cause of my child's illness?

Years from now, it might be clear why something happened to you. It's part of a grand plan that we may not comprehend during our time on Earth. You can't change what happened, and you might never find out why until you've returned to the Spirit world.

Whatever happens, whether it is a blessing or a curse, you must accept it and move on. Don't let it take control of your life.

Live with Peace

Isn't it more manageable to be calm rather than stressed out? Of course that is the case. Therefore, make the decision to be peaceful. It appears straightforward because it is. Make the conscious decision to pursue peace in every circumstance. Many people react negatively to novel circumstances, which causes them to deviate from their typical patterns of behavior.

Instead of resisting or arguing against the changes that are occurring in your life, choose to accept them peacefully. Most of the time, there is nothing you can do to alter the current circumstances.

Everything That Arises Passes Away

One day or another, every life will end, whether it be before or after yours. You will pass on to the light source, as will your family and children, your friends and acquaintances, your pets, and even your plants and flowers. Everyone in your household will eventually reach the light source. It's okay. It's unavoidable; that's just how life is. Because of this, we might as well make the decision to go through life with elegance, tranquility, and a sense of playfulness. If you choose the alternative, you will find that your life is filled with struggle, monotony, and conflict. Make this decision daily.

Flow with Life

Live life following your intuition. How many times have you had a hunch that you should be doing something or going in a different direction, but you decided not to follow that hunch only to realize that it would have made a difference in your life? Learn to follow hunches. Flow with the inner thoughts that you know are right for you, going with life's current rather than fighting it.

Listen to your Spirit guides. They are leading you on the right path. They are the voice in your head, helping you to make the best decisions. Not only is it the right path, but it's also the peaceful path in your life. Run your life on Spiritual energy, not recommendations from those who don't understand you and your life path.

Love

Always carry the feeling of love within your heart. Love should be given out freely to all people and all things. Everyone, including humans and animals, craves affection and companionship. This demonstrates how significant love is.

The emotion of love is something that everyone has experienced, whether it be love for a significant other in their life, love for a child or parent, or love for a pet. It is the most amazing sensation there is, both in this world and all others. Therefore, make it a habit to send love everywhere, even to those unfortunate beings who are incapable of feeling anything but rage and releasing it into the world. Send your love to them. It will have a significant impact your life as well as theirs.

Life Is an Illusion

Is this a true-life experience?

It feels genuine right down to the second. But who are we if we are simply light energy having a human experience? This is the question we should think about every day. Who exactly are we? What exactly are we? What is the purpose of the light energy that keeps us alive? What is the point of having a human experience? There is a clear reason for this, which some of us may not realize until our light energy moves on to the next dimension.

Many people, however, have discovered it through deep, inquisitive thought and meditation. These are the people who live their lives with ease, knowing that they are accomplishing on Earth what the source sent them here to do. As a result, they understand that life is an illusion. They understand that they are only here for a limited time to help humanity in a unique way and that only they have the ability to do so. As a result, death is also an illusion to them, and they have no need to be concerned about life and death. Your life force energy lasts forever.

Choose Happiness

It sounds simple, and it is if you train your mind. We encounter a wide range of emotions, from happiness to anger to sadness to elation and everything in between, sometimes in a short span of time.

It is your choice to live your life in the emotion you choose. You can choose to be angry all the time and live a life of anger, upsetting everyone you encounter and making yourself and others miserable. But why? Why would anyone choose to live a life of anger? It's often because we don't understand. Such people don't understand that the choice is theirs.

Life on Earth is too short to live in anger when happiness is also a choice. When you are happy, you make others happy, including yourself. The happier you choose to be, the happier you become, and it becomes a habit. It is easier said than done, but like any other habit, it becomes a practice.

There are plenty of excuses to not see happiness as a possibility because of daily changes and life experiences, like illness, poverty, depression, tragic accidents, and even the death of friends and loved ones. Have you encountered angry, depressed people with great wealth? Have you encountered happy people with no money at all? Likewise, angry people claim they are that way because they lost all their money and never had anything, to begin with. There are folks who have lost their entire families in tragic accidents yet choose to be happy. Choose happiness.

Meditate

There is nothing more important in this life experience than quiet reflection into your soul. Quieting your mind allows you to live the truths of the Spirit world. This is also the key to realizing why you have a human experience. What is your mission to accomplish on Earth? What special gift do you have that can help all of mankind? No one else has this special gift but you. It is up to you to share it with the world.

A form of quiet reflection, be it prayer or meditation, will allow you to find your Spiritual gift. There are many forms of self-reflection. Choose one that is comfortable for you and use it every day. The world is waiting for you to share your gift and help mankind.

Take a Breath

Thank you for taking the time to read Spirit Gift. If you got this far you may have interest in the content or how to improve your life and the lives of your friends, family, and co-worker team. I want to continue to help.

I kept all my publishing rights for this reason. Let's help each other. Here's how:

1. Amazon reviews are important. If you liked the book even a little, please take a few seconds to give the book a review.
2. Share it with a friend.
3. If you need multiple copies, I can assist with discounted bulk orders
4. If your team needs to "Take a breath", I'd gladly speak at your event and share the principles behind Spirit Gift.

Let's stay in contact:

jeff@jeffwellman.com

SpiritGift.net

facebook.com/Jeffwellman2100

instagram.com/SpiritGiftBook/?next=%2F

linkedin.com/in/jeff-wellman-632a2a15/

Take a breath.

Made in United States
Troutdale, OR
09/16/2024